Cloak and Grammar

Allie Pleiter

AnniesFiction.com

Books in the Secrets of the Castleton Manor Library series

Library of Congress-in-Publication Data
Cloak and Grammar / by Allie Pleiter
p. cm.
I. Title
                    2018961928

AnniesFiction.com
(800) 282-6643
Secrets of the Castleton Manor Library™
Series Creator: Shari Lohner
Series Editor: Lorie Jones
Cover Illustrator: Jesse Reisch

10 11 12 13 14 | Printed in China | 9 8 7 6 5 4 3

Faith Newberry pulled in a deep breath of salty ocean air. "Well, Watson, evidently insomnia has its benefits," she told her black-and-white tuxedo cat as they walked across the wide lawn of Castleton Manor where she worked. The nineteenth-century estate was famous for attracting booklovers and their pets from around the world.

The sun came up over the Atlantic Ocean just beyond the manor, spreading a palette of colors across the sky that was worthy of the finest oil painting.

"Look at that spectacular sunrise," she said.

Watson padded along beside her, clearly taking no notice of the beautiful pastel scene.

Faith hadn't really expected him to appreciate the view. After all, cats were mostly nocturnal, and Watson had never quite warmed to an early bird mentality.

"I get it," she said with a yawn, glad for the cool sea breeze in what had been a hot and humid June. "I'd rather be asleep too. If my insomnia continues, I'll be on my last nerve by the time this event is over."

Tomorrow would begin author Red Maxton's retirement celebration, organized by his longtime publisher. The author boasted two dozen best-selling Trey Connor spy novels and a series of movies. Red's most ardent fans would gather to celebrate the end of his popular series with talks, parties, and special exhibitions.

As Faith turned toward the manor's grand front entrance, she decided to ask Iris Alden, who ran the manor's coffee and gift shop, for her strongest brew. And the largest cup. It was going to take a big dose of caffeine to keep her awake for all the preparations ahead of her today.

She was dreaming of a steaming triple-shot latte with extra whipped cream when a sharp yell cut through the morning mist.

It was followed by another shout and something that sounded very much like a man's voice crying, "Help!"

"Who's there?" she asked as she spun toward the noise.

As the shouting continued, Faith took off toward the manor's hedge maze at a run, Watson bounding at her heels. "I'm coming!" she yelled as she headed into the labyrinth of boxwoods, thankful she knew the layout of the garden puzzle.

"Miss Newberry?"

Faith recognized the voice. It was Eban Matthews, one of the manor's gardeners. "Eban?" she called as she rounded another corner. "Is that you? Where are you?"

"The south corner!" Eban hollered through the shrubbery. "Hurry!"

Faith skidded to a stop on the stone pavers and reversed direction.

Watson, obviously deciding humans ran much too slowly, took advantage of his size by ducking straight into the plants.

A shortcut through the hedges might have been possible for Watson, but Faith was forced to follow the winding paths. She tried to run faster, but she tripped as her heel caught in the grass between two pavers. "Are you hurt?"

"No, I'm okay," Eban answered. "But . . ."

Faith yanked her shoe out of the turf and ran on. "What is it?"

"More like who," Eban replied. "I think he's—oh no, this isn't good."

"Is it Mack?" Faith asked. The manor's elderly maintenance man had endured more than his share of back problems this year. She hated to think of him coming to any kind of harm. He was a fixture at Castleton, and everyone was fond of him.

"No, it's not Mack. I don't know who this is."

Faith finally made it around the last corner. Stopping to catch her breath, she silently took in the scene.

Watson had already arrived, and he was sitting down next to Eban. The young man was staring at two legs protruding from the base of the hedge. A pair of men's brown leather shoes, motionless, confirmed what Eban had said. Someone—a stranger or a manor guest, evidently—was lying unconscious or worse at the base of the hedge maze.

Faith lost no time springing into action. "Help me pull him out."

Eban shook his head. "I tried that already. He's stuck in there pretty good. That's the thickest part of the maze wall."

"Sir?" Faith tried shaking one of the legs, alarmed at the cold and wet material. "His clothes are soaked."

"And it stopped raining hours ago." Eban swallowed hard. "I don't think he's asleep or passed out."

Faith pushed up one pant leg and touched the man's ankle. Her stomach roiled at the chilly, damp sensation. The man was dead or close to it. "I have to say I agree."

Despite Eban's comments, Faith felt compelled to try to pull the man free on the remote chance he was still alive. She hauled on the legs with all her might but discovered the man to be as firmly wedged in the shrubbery as Eban had told her. "Did you call an ambulance?"

"I was just getting out my phone to do that," Eban said.

"Go ahead and call. Then see if you can shove these boxwood trunks apart so we can get him out of there." She pushed the pant leg up again and examined the bluish tint of the pale and icy skin. Was there a spot on an ankle to check for a pulse?

From what she could see, Faith was afraid the man was already gone. "Any idea who this could be? I didn't think we had any guests checked in for the Red Maxton event yet. But if he's not a guest, then who is he? And what is he doing in the maze?"

Eban shrugged. "Beats me." He called 911 and reported the incident to the dispatcher.

Faith stood and removed her own cell phone from her pocket. She needed to alert Wolfe Jaxon, the co-owner of the manor, about the situation. She had to admit that she was also eager to hear his soothing voice.

She checked the time—five thirty. If Wolfe wasn't already awake, he would be soon. She couldn't imagine Wolfe would welcome starting his Friday morning by learning there was a dead body in his family estate's hedge maze, but there was no helping it.

Eban finished talking to the dispatcher and slid his phone into his pocket. "Help is on the way."

"If you're up to it, see if you can part those branches over there," Faith suggested. "We might be able to get him out that way."

"I'll try," Eban said, then struggled through the boxwood's thick tangle of branches.

Watson followed. His stub of a tail was the last thing Faith saw before the cat disappeared inside the hedge. It was the result of an injury he'd suffered as a kitten living on the streets in Boston before Faith had taken him in.

Taking a deep breath to gain a shred more composure, Faith called Wolfe.

"Still not sleeping well?" Wolfe's voice was thick with slumber as he came on the line. A frequent world traveler, Wolfe had given Faith several suggestions on how to kick her recent bout of insomnia, but none had met with success.

"Yes, but that's not why I woke you."

"You didn't," Wolfe replied, although his drowsy tone made Faith suspect he was simply being nice. "I'm usually up at this hour anyway. Is everything all right?"

Faith watched the bushes rustle as Eban made another attempt to dislodge the man. "Not exactly. In fact, not at all. I'm with Eban in the hedge maze, and you should get down here right away."

"The hedge maze? At this hour?"

"Eban discovered a man stuck in the maze," Faith explained. "I can only see his legs, but he seems to be unconscious—"

"I'll be right there," Wolfe cut in, his voice fully alert now. Rustling sounds in the background made Faith think he was pulling on clothes at a fast pace. "Have you called 911?"

"Yes, Eban did," Faith answered.

She heard Wolfe's apartment door click in the background and then his footsteps as he ran down the manor's carpeted stairs from the third floor where his private residence was.

"Any idea who he is?" Wolfe asked.

"I can't even see him, except his shoes," Faith admitted.

"What kind of shoes is he wearing?" Wolfe asked. "Running shoes? Hiking boots?"

"They're brown leather shoes. They appear fairly large, so I'd guess he's a tall fellow." Faith swallowed hard before adding, "Or was."

"Let's say he is until we know for sure to say otherwise," Wolfe responded. "What else do you see?"

Faith surveyed the man's footwear. "He's wearing red polka-dot socks. You don't see those very often."

Even fashionable footwear didn't narrow things down much. Given the manor's appeal for books and pets, manor guests were frequently academics and literary fans, who sometimes dressed in costumes in honor of their favorite authors and fictional characters.

But we have no guests yet, Faith reminded herself. *The Maxton affair won't start for another day.*

"Anything else?" Wolfe persisted.

Faith scanned the scene, mentally cataloging anything that could be used as a clue. "His clothes are wet, which means he was out here in last night's rain."

"I thought we didn't have any guests for the Maxton event yet," Wolfe said.

"That's what I thought. I'm totally stumped as to who this man might be." Faith tried to peer through the thick shrubbery, but she couldn't see anything clearly, and she couldn't get any closer. Eban had practically climbed the branches to get in as far as he had.

"He's pushed in here pretty good," Eban said from inside the boxwoods. "It makes me think someone tried to hide him and gave up when he didn't quite fit."

What did it take to wedge a lifeless body so far into the hedge? If the size of the man's feet was any indication, he was tall and possibly hefty.

"Oh no," Eban said. "I'm pretty sure he's dead."

Faith had already come to that conclusion. After all, as relaxing as it was to be a guest at Castleton Manor, no one took to napping in the shrubbery. Especially overnight in the rain.

"I'm out the door," Wolfe said, and she could hear the crunch of stones as he ran across the manor's broad circular drive.

"What do you see?" Faith asked Eban. "Describe him for me."

More branches and leaves shook, and Eban said, "I think he's about Mr. Jaxon's age. Stockier, though."

Faith told herself to think like Police Chief Andy Garris. She'd had neither enough coffee nor sleep to do this well, but that couldn't matter. "White male, midforties, heavy to medium build," she relayed into the phone.

"He's at least six feet tall," Eban went on. The legs in front of her lurched as Eban made another attempt to untangle the body from the hedge. "And he's not going anywhere. He's kind of stiff."

"Where are you in the maze?" Wolfe asked.

"South corner," Faith answered. "Hurry."

"I'm coming." This time, his voice echoed. He was close enough that she didn't need the phone to hear him.

As Faith disconnected the call, the wail of an ambulance siren cut through the misty quiet.

In a matter of seconds, Wolfe appeared from around the corner.

He wore jeans and a hastily donned sweater, and his hair was mussed. But his alarmed expression showed that he was wide-awake.

"Eban?" Wolfe asked, pushing his way into the hedge. He all but ran into the gardener as the young man emerged from the branches.

Eban's face was as white as the pale clouds that decorated the sky. "He's dead. There's a dead man in our hedge."

"I know," Wolfe said soothingly. "We'll figure out what happened."

"I found this." Eban held up a playing card, the three of diamonds. "It was in his hand. There was a gun in his other hand, but I wasn't going to touch that."

Faith knew that he shouldn't have touched the card either, but poor Eban looked as if he might keel over at any second.

"Definitely don't touch that gun," Wolfe said. "Why don't I take the card?"

Eban handed it to him.

Wolfe slipped the card into his pocket, then rested a hand on Eban's shoulder. "You go out to the entrance of the maze and guide in the ambulance, all right? Faith and I will handle it from here."

Faith admired the fact that Wolfe took a personal interest in every one of the manor's employees, treating each one as a valued member of the team that kept the manor running smoothly. He had taken a particular liking to the enterprising young gardener, helping him advance his career and education whenever he could.

Eban nodded and walked away.

Wolfe gave Faith a worried glance, then pushed into the foliage where Eban had just been. "So, no idea who the man is?"

"None," Faith repeated. "But the playing card . . ." She recalled the research she'd done earlier this week. International spy hero Trey Connor was Red's claim to fame. Every story in the best-selling series featured exotic locales, fancy cars, global intrigue, amazing gadgets, and the spy's signature—the three of diamonds.

Faith had read that the spy gave the playing card to women as a remembrance, placed it on the villains he vanquished, and left it behind whenever he disappeared into the night at the end of each novel. It was quite literally Trey Connor's calling card.

The three of diamonds could only mean that this—whatever this was—had to be connected to the event somehow.

"The three of diamonds is Trey Connor's signature," Faith said.

"You're right," Wolfe said. "The card can't be good news."

Faith gazed up at the sky. "When is finding a body in your hedge maze ever anything but bad news?"

Wolfe merely grunted in reply.

At that moment, Watson appeared from underneath the branches. "Where have you been?" Faith asked him.

The cat didn't answer. Instead, he strolled away toward the manor.

Wolfe exited the hedge with much less ease than Watson, his expression somewhere between worry and fear.

"What is it?" Faith said.

"The man has red hair," Wolfe said. "I'm sorry to say that thanks to their being wide open, I can tell you he has green eyes." He seemed to place great importance on those facts.

"And?" Faith prompted.

"Don't forget he was carrying a three of diamonds." Wolfe held up the playing card that Eban had found. "And he's wearing a blue bow tie."

Faith stared at Wolfe. He had just described Trey Connor. She attempted to push the branches aside to peer through the leaves, but she couldn't see anything. "Trey Connor isn't real. He can't be lying dead in the hedge maze."

As she let the thick branches of tiny oval leaves fall back into place, Chief Garris rounded the corner with Officers Mick Tobin and Bryan Laddy and a team of paramedics. Eban was right behind them.

"Trey Connor?" one of the paramedics repeated. "He's dead in your hedge maze?"

"Of course not," Wolfe said. "But unless I'm mistaken, Red Maxton is."

Faith gasped. "That's Red Maxton in the maze?"

Wolfe scratched his chin. "I think so. The man has red hair, green eyes, a blue bow tie, and Eban said he was holding a three of diamonds."

With a nod from Chief Garris, one paramedic pushed his way through the foliage, presumably to check for a pulse.

A few seconds later, the paramedic returned and shook his head. "This victim is deceased. Five or six hours, I'd guess."

Eban pulled something up on his phone, then faced the screen out to show a publicity photo of the famous author. "That's him. That's the guy."

Faith studied the photograph. It was similar to a dozen she'd seen in her research for the upcoming celebration. Red Maxton was wearing a white dinner jacket and a blue bow tie, and he stood beside a fancy car. The redheaded man flashed a smile as he held both an oversize three of diamonds playing card and a copy of his most recent Trey Connor novel.

Even with the photograph, Faith couldn't confirm the identity of the man in the hedge because she could only view his shoes and socks.

The serious looks that passed between Wolfe and Eban, however, left little to no doubt. That was Red Maxton in there, and he was dead.

Insufficient sleep had become the least of her problems.

An impulse to push her way into the hedge to see for herself warred with a sense that she'd rather not add the sight of the dead body to her memories. "But how? Red's not even supposed to be here yet. No one is."

"Well, I doubt he was supposed to be dead either," Laddy said.

The chief shot the officer a glare.

Faith turned in a slow circle, one hand on her forehead, mulling over the implications of the morning's grim discovery. "The retirement party starts tomorrow, and we just found our guest of honor dead in the hedge maze."

"So you didn't know Mr. Maxton was here?" Garris asked, opening his ever-present notepad and clicking the top of his pen. "And by here, I mean in Lighthouse Bay, not"—he nodded toward the feet now ominously protruding from the leaves—"here in your hedge maze."

Wolfe frowned and shook his head.

"Red, his editor, and some others were scheduled to arrive this afternoon," Faith said. "The rest of the guests are coming tomorrow."

"Red's editor is on a two o'clock train from New York, along with a small group of event leaders arriving by car later today," Wolfe added.

"How was Mr. Maxton arriving?" the chief asked.

"Red and his Airedale terrier, Rufus, were driving on their own," Faith responded. "I believe they were coming from Vermont."

Tobin glanced around. "Any sign of the dog?"

The thought of Red's confused terrier roaming the estate in search of his deceased master pulled at Faith's heartstrings. Had Rufus been out in last night's storm? "Eban and I didn't see a dog, but even a loyal animal might wander around if . . ." She let her voice trail off.

It might be time to call Midge Foster, Faith's good friend and the concierge vet for the manor. Midge would surely know the best way to locate and comfort the poor animal with his master gone.

Garris scribbled in his notepad. "We've had no calls for a missing person here, and I can check Vermont. But based on what you told me, neither Mr. Maxton's publishing staff nor anyone else would have reason to suspect him missing yet."

"If he was traveling alone, I suppose not," Wolfe said. "Do we know if he had any family?"

"I don't remember reading about any. In Red's official biography, it listed only his beloved dog," Faith replied. "But many authors are private about their personal lives and families, so he might have someone."

"What about identification?" the chief asked. "Did anyone find a wallet or a cell phone?"

"I'm sorry, but I didn't think to search," Eban admitted. "I only saw the playing card and the gun."

"You did fine," Wolfe told him. "After you give your statement to Chief Garris, I want you to take the rest of the day off."

"If it's all the same to you, I'd prefer to stay," Eban said. "I'm going to need something to do to shake this off. I don't want to spend the rest of today sitting at home wondering about it."

Faith checked her watch. Her good friend Brooke Milner was the head chef at the manor, and she should already be at work preparing for the day. There weren't many stresses in the world that couldn't be alleviated by Brooke's wonderful cooking.

"Why don't I text Brooke and ask her to cook a good breakfast for you?" Faith suggested to Eban. "Then you can decide whether to stay or go home."

"Great idea," Wolfe said.

Faith typed out a short version of the information and her request and sent it to Brooke.

Anything to help, Brooke replied promptly.

We'll send him over in a few minutes, Faith texted. *He's rattled. Take care of him.*

Will do. Tough break. Come by the kitchen when you can.

Faith thanked Brooke, then faced the others. "It's all settled, Eban. So now what do we do?" She felt the question press down on her weary shoulders. The death of a beloved author—the death of anyone, for that matter—was a tragedy. "This has some huge consequences."

"Many of Red's most loyal fans are due here in less than twenty-four hours," Wolfe said. "And they're expecting a celebration."

"We can't exactly revise Red Maxton's retirement celebration into the man's wake," Faith said. "At least I hope no one gets such a macabre idea."

Garris took charge. "The first thing we need to do is finish our site investigation so we can get the poor man out of your hedge."

"I tried to move him before I realized he was dead," Eban offered sheepishly, as if the hedge's reluctance to release the body were somehow his fault as a gardener. "He's stuck in there pretty good." He shuffled his feet on the stone pavers. "And he's stiff."

"Don't you worry," the chief reassured him. "Officers Tobin and Laddy will take care of the details. Would you fetch some shears or something to cut away the branches before you go? I think we're going to have to hack away a fair bit of the hedge to get Mr. Maxton out. Sorry about that, by the way. I know you do a lot to keep them looking this nice."

"I understand, sir," Eban said, clearly grateful for something concrete to do. With a nod to Wolfe, the young man set off through the maze.

"That's a tough thing to get over," Garris remarked when Eban was out of earshot. He scanned the scene. "Nothing else out of place? Benches knocked over, signs of a struggle, that sort of thing?"

Wolfe studied the elegant surroundings. "I'll have Eban inspect the area more closely, but nothing appears out of place to me. Faith?"

One of the perks of Faith's post as the manor librarian was her residence in the charming gardener's cottage, so she knew the grounds well.

She glanced around the maze and noticed nothing amiss. "Not that I can see from here." Her gaze roamed to the unfortunate feet protruding from the leaves. "Between you and me, I'm having trouble imagining how he got in that thick hedge in the first place."

"There's an exit wound in the man's abdomen," the chief said. "There may be a gun in Mr. Maxton's hand, but I doubt he shot himself and then crawled into the hedge."

Faith gasped. "So you're saying it's murder?" She could have had a month of restful sleep and still not have been ready to face this today.

Garris adjusted his hat and squinted into the rising sun. "Did anyone report hearing a gunshot or a loud noise?"

"Not that I know of," Wolfe replied.

"A gunshot could have gone completely unnoticed during the thunderstorm last night," Faith reasoned.

The chief turned to Tobin and Laddy. "The bullet exited the body, so it may still be around. I'll collect the weapon. You two survey the maze for the bullet, shell, or anything else."

The pair of officers set about their task.

Garris put on a pair of gloves. "I've handled a lot of unusual cases in my career, but I believe this is the first time I've had to extract a famous author from a hedge maze."

Wolfe cringed. "It never crossed my mind to add that particular distinction to your experience."

"Can you pull up that photo Eban had on your phone?" the chief asked. "Let's get another comparison while I search the body for identification."

Wolfe took out his phone and searched for the photo.

"We'd better tell Marlene so we can start figuring out what to do about tomorrow," Faith said. Marlene Russell was the assistant manager of the manor and one of the most efficient people Faith knew. Still, Faith was sure the problem that now lay ahead of the manor staff would vex even Marlene's considerable organizational talents. "We'll have to cancel, I'm sure."

Garris exited the hedge with a sleek pistol inside a plastic evidence bag. "It's anyone's guess whether or not this will have any viable prints besides his on it."

"Did you find any personal effects?" Faith asked.

"Whoever did it stripped him of his ID," the chief answered. "I found no wallet, no car keys, and no cell phone."

"But he's a celebrity," Wolfe reminded Garris. "His face is all the identification we need."

"It's not quite that simple, though he does have a distinctive face," the chief responded. "I'd say we can be 90 percent sure the man in there is your Red Maxton."

Faith slumped down onto a nearby bench. "That's terrible news."

Garris sealed the evidence bag containing what for now had to be considered the murder weapon. "The question is, who do we call? I don't think a dog counts as next of kin, and we don't even know where his dog is."

"We may be able to help with that," Wolfe said. "We have his editor's number in Marlene's files. We've been working with him to coordinate everything. His name is Nick Westfield."

The chief handed the evidence bag to Tobin, then turned to Wolfe. "You'd better take me up to your office so we can make the call. Trey Connor—or at least the man who wrote him—has been dealt his final card."

"That was awful," Marlene moaned as she disconnected the phone.

Faith would have to count the long and difficult call she, Marlene, and Wolfe had just made to Red's editor as one of the worst of her career.

Chief Garris had made the initial notification to Nick Westfield that his star author was almost certainly dead and likely murdered. The editor was shocked and grief-stricken at the news. Who wouldn't be? It would have been a terrible turn of events under any circumstances, but with a major event less than a day away, it was promising to be both tragic and chaotic.

Wolfe had offered to call Nick back in an hour, but the editor surprised Faith by insisting they all stay on the line. "The best thing I can do is start figuring out our next steps," Nick told them.

The editor was right in some respects. Despite the devastating news, the guests were preparing to travel. Quick action was necessary.

Faith felt her heart twist to hear the anguish and shock in Nick's voice as the man wrestled with what to do. Twice he had to pause the conversation to regain his composure. Finally, he decided to cancel the whole thing, and they hung up.

When Marlene sank back into her office chair in an uncharacteristic show of discomfort, Faith could hardly blame her.

"That was certainly one of the more difficult calls I've ever made on behalf of Castleton," Wolfe agreed.

"There wasn't really anything else we could do," Faith said.

"Nick was our only contact," Marlene replied. "And we had to make a decision regarding the event. It had to be done."

If there was ever a woman whose life motto was doing what had to be done, Faith thought it was Marlene.

The assistant manager took a deep breath, then picked up the file labeled *Maxton Party* from where it lay open on her desk. "I'll call a staff meeting in thirty minutes. Then we can begin working with Nick to notify the guests." She nodded at Wolfe. "I'm sure they'll appreciate your gesture of waiving the cancellation fees."

"It seemed like the least we could do," he said.

"We'll take a hit with all those vacancies." Marlene studied the large calendar on her wall. "It's our high season."

"We'll manage," Wolfe assured her.

While Wolfe had proven himself an astute and successful businessman, he always put people ahead of profits. Faith admired that about him.

"It broke my heart how Nick asked if we were sure it was Red and if we'd found Rufus." Faith had hated telling Nick that the dog had yet to appear, but she tried to console him by saying she was sure that if any of the kind residents of Lighthouse Bay had found him wandering around in the rain, they would have taken him in immediately.

"If there is anyone personal to notify, I'm sure Nick will take it from here," Wolfe said. "Now that the event is canceled, we can take the next steps." He stood up. "Marlene, what can I do to help?"

"I'll help too," Faith offered. "Whatever you need."

Marlene clicked into action, her natural efficiency returning as she ticked off tasks on her fingers. "Food orders and the staff schedule will have to be scaled back. We'll need to contact all the known reservations within the hour, if we can."

"E-mail me the list, and I'll take care of that," Wolfe said. "In fact, I think I'll do personal calls offering our guests a 30 percent discount if they'd still like to come and enjoy the manor and the weather. If these people have taken time off work or out of their lives, maybe the best thing is to give them somewhere beautiful to go."

Marlene gaped at him. "And have the man's fans come to gawk at the hedge maze where he spent his final hours?"

"Of course not. Garris has closed off the maze as a crime scene. Do your best to hold off until the end of the day to scale back the food orders and staff schedules. I should have talked to enough guests to get a sense of our bookings by then."

Marlene nodded.

As Faith walked with Wolfe up the stairs from Marlene's lower-level office, Faith yawned. It was still early, but already the day felt weeks long.

"Have you eaten yet?" Wolfe asked as they passed the enormous dining room on the main floor.

The enticing scents of coffee and bacon wafting into the lobby roused a grumble from Faith's stomach. "I had some yogurt at home." She yawned again. "But nowhere near enough coffee."

Wolfe took her hand and redirected her toward the small breakfast room. "Let's remedy that. I don't think either of us should handle today without a good breakfast. Fifteen minutes and a plate of scrambled eggs won't damage our action plan."

Faith smiled. "I can't argue with that logic."

Wolfe pulled the chair out for her. He arranged for a quick breakfast for the two of them and asked the server to send a plate to Marlene in her office.

"That's kind of you," Faith said as Wolfe sat down.

"I can't remember when Marlene's been more rattled," Wolfe responded. "It's not much, but it might help her face the rest of today."

While they waited for their food to arrive, Faith and Wolfe gazed out the window at the beautiful view of the ocean.

"You're right," Faith said, gesturing at the picturesque scene. "Maybe several of the guests would still like to come and stay despite Red being gone."

"I'd never make the offer just to fill the rooms," Wolfe said. "This is the place I'll always come to when I need to get my feet back underneath me. Why not for them as well?"

Castleton Manor had been in the Jaxon family for more than a century, and Wolfe had grown up there. He was a direct descendant of Angus Jaxon, the wealthy shipowner and whaling captain who had built the magnificent building in the late 1800s.

Faith had to admit the grand estate and the cottage she shared with Watson had come to feel like home to her as well. Besides her wonderful house, she had so much to be thankful for—all her friends in Lighthouse Bay, her loyal cat, the exquisite books in her care, and the kind man now sitting across the table from her.

Faith took Wolfe's hand, grateful that no matter what chaos life threw at her, she knew she could count on her friends and family to help see her through.

Her peaceful thoughts were interrupted by a large black-and-tan dog barking and romping across the lawn right under the window.

It wasn't unusual to see pets at the manor with their masters. But this dog not only lacked a leash, but it seemed to be without an owner.

When she recognized the breed, Faith caught her breath. "That's an Airedale." She pointed to the dog now running in circles. "I think it's Red Maxton's dog, Rufus."

They both jumped up and hurried to the window.

A tennis ball sailed into view, and the dog dashed after it. If the dog was Red's, he seemed joyfully oblivious to his owner's fate.

"What on earth is going on?" Wolfe rushed into the next room and out onto the balcony overlooking the yard.

Faith followed him, wondering what they would do if they caught the dog.

Her wonder evaporated into shock when she glimpsed what had already stopped Wolfe in his tracks.

A tall, red-haired, green-eyed man wearing a blue bow tie rubbed the dog's ears. "Good boy, Rufus."

Red Maxton stood alive and well on the lawn.

3

"It's you!" Faith exclaimed as she burst out onto the terrace.

The man spread his arms wide, beaming. "Red Maxton, in the flesh."

Faith swallowed hard at the man's all-too-poignant choice of words.

"What's the matter?" Red glanced from Faith to Wolfe. "You knew I was showing up today, right?"

Rufus dropped the tennis ball at his owner's feet and gave a jubilant bark.

Red leaned down to pet the dog. "Nice place you've got here. And I love that I can bring Rufus along."

Wolfe walked toward the author, obviously regaining his composure a bit faster than Faith was able to. "Thank you. I'm Wolfe Jaxon, the manor's co-owner. Please come and sit down for a minute."

Red commanded Rufus to follow as he went with Faith and Wolfe to the breakfast room. "People usually seem much happier to see me, if you don't mind my saying so," he joked as he sat at the table.

"Oh, we're delighted you're here," Faith said. "It's just that . . ." She trailed off and shot a pleading glance for help at Wolfe.

"We have some unusual circumstances at the moment." Wolfe took a deep breath. With an impressively calm tone, he relayed the events of the morning.

Faith watched as the author's cavalier demeanor became more and more alarmed.

"Like me?" Red's deep voice pitched higher, and his eyes widened.

"I'm afraid so," Wolfe replied.

Red rose and began to pace the room. "You're telling me someone who looks exactly like me was murdered right here mere hours ago? How am I supposed to take that as anything other than a threat on my life? The killer, whoever he was, obviously thought he was shooting me."

"That is one theory." Wolfe gestured for Red to sit back down. "I know this is upsetting, but let's try to think rationally about it. We don't really know enough to make assumptions at this point. Mr. Westfield—"

"You've talked to Nick?" Red interrupted.

Faith nodded. "He was very upset to hear about what we thought was your demise." She couldn't find a better way to word the absurd situation. "He canceled the retirement party."

"He canceled?" Red exclaimed. "Without talking to me?" Then the reality of it seemed to strike him, and he softened his voice. "Well, yes, I suppose he didn't think he could talk to me."

Faith poured the distressed man a cup of coffee. "What would you like us to do?"

Red took the coffee and downed it in nearly a single gulp. He all but slammed the cup back on the table. "For a start, triple your security."

"So you want to go ahead with the party?" Wolfe asked.

"No. Yes." Red buried his face in his hands. "I don't know."

For a moment, Faith could see that the larger-than-life persona Red showed the world might not be the man's true nature.

"The murderer is out there," Red continued, still in a state of high agitation. "And who in the blazes is that man inside your hedge?"

That's the question of the hour, Faith thought.

"Like I said, there's a great deal that we don't yet know," Wolfe responded.

Red pinched the bridge of his nose and was quiet for a long time. Then he reached into his pocket and pulled out his cell phone. "I'm calling Nick. We've got to figure this out."

Faith gulped, thinking Nick Westfield was about to get the most shocking call of his life.

"So, they decided to go through with Red's retirement celebration after all?" Faith's aunt Eileen put down her knitting as they sat outside on one of the manor's terraces later that day.

The sweet older woman had come to share an afternoon coffee with Faith. Together they sipped Iris's delicious coffee creations while they watched a dozen high-end sports cars being lined up on the grass beyond the estate's sweeping drive.

Faith had just recounted the horror of finding the dead man who resembled Red Maxton in the hedge maze and then the shock of Red himself showing up at the manor, very much alive.

"I'm as stunned as you are," Faith said. "Red seemed genuinely afraid for his life, and I can't blame him. I thought they'd definitely cancel."

After Faith and Wolfe had informed Marlene of the shocking twist, the three of them had conferred with Red and Nick. The author and the editor had eventually decided to continue as planned.

"They do say that everyone has a double somewhere in the world," Eileen remarked as she resumed her knitting.

Faith stroked Watson as he soaked up the summer sun while napping on her lap. "But a double right here in Lighthouse Bay? It's uncanny and kind of scary, don't you think?"

"What if it's not a double in that sense?" Eileen asked. "What if it's more like an impersonator? There are plenty of those to imitate celebrities at parties and such. I've seen them on television."

Faith gave her aunt a doubtful look. "Movie stars, maybe. I could possibly imagine it for the actor who plays Trey Connor in the movies. But for an author? Do you really think there are enough people who know who Red Maxton is to warrant hiring an impersonator? Or murdering one?"

Eileen nodded. "You're right. It doesn't really make sense. Then again, all your guests are paying a pretty penny to come here and celebrate Red's retirement. And these cars are quite expensive. Maybe wealthy people are used to splurges like hired impersonators."

"Even if that's true, then who was in the maze?" Faith countered. So far, no one had an explanation for that, least of all Red.

"Trey Connor in disguise?" Eileen teased. "After all, he carried the three of diamonds, didn't he?"

"Why are you the second person today I've had to remind that Trey Connor isn't a real person?" Faith was glad to laugh a bit, but the laugh dissolved into a weary yawn.

Eileen paused her knitting and studied her niece's face. "Are you still having trouble sleeping?"

"I was up at four," Faith admitted. "Iris's coffee helps, but I think I'd be far better off if I could nap like my assistant here." She motioned to Watson, who was softly snoring.

"Oh, I think we'd all be happier if we could nap like Watson." Eileen returned to her stitching. "So, if I'm the second person you had to remind of Trey Connor's fictional status, who was the first?"

"Wolfe. He made a remark about it being Trey Connor they found in the hedge since the spy has red hair like his creator."

Eileen gave a knowing smile. "And how are things with Wolfe?" Faith's aunt—along with her other friends—never hid the fact that they had matched Faith and Wolfe up long before she would openly admit her feelings for him.

Faith sighed. "We're dating. He's my boss. It's complicated." This was becoming her standard answer for the many inquiries Faith fielded on the subject.

Thankfully, her friends were supportive and encouraging of their relationship. At first, Marlene had seemed to disapprove, but lately Faith had noticed that the assistant manager appeared to have come to terms with it.

"You seem happy," Eileen offered. "Tired but happy."

Faith leaned back in the chair. "I am. He's so charming. And there's his business mogul elegance. But at the same time, he's not at all pretentious or stuffy. He's simply wonderful."

Her aunt's smile warmed even more. "You two are good for each other, and you deserve to be happy. When there aren't bodies lurking in your shrubbery, that is." She turned her knitting and shook her head. "I can't imagine."

"Some days I wonder what he sees in me." Faith gestured to the expensive vehicles. "He owns cars like those. He lives in this luxurious estate and regularly travels to exotic locales. Me? I'm a librarian. Shouldn't he be with a supermodel or a movie star or something?"

"Don't you dare forget that you're beautiful in dozens of ways that don't show up on magazine covers or bank accounts," Eileen admonished. "And I've seen how Wolfe gazes at you. He definitely considers you beautiful."

"Are compliments like that in the favorite aunt's handbook?" Faith teased.

"Something like that," Eileen replied with a grin. "As for exotic locales, I imagine they're nice to visit, but nothing ever beats a warm home with a family who loves you."

"You're right," Faith responded. "Wolfe said something today about the manor being the place where he returns when he needs to regain his footing."

"I can understand that."

Faith regarded the imposing house. With its angled roofs, stone walls, and ornate architecture, it resembled a fairy-tale castle. She had a hard time thinking of it as a childhood home full of warm memories. Yet Wolfe had told her story after story of his happy childhood years growing up within the lavish rooms.

"No matter how big or small it is, a home is always home," Eileen said, as if she knew what her niece was thinking. After a moment, she gave Faith a quizzical look. "So why do you still seem worried?"

"This morning, I thought there was a dead author in the hedge maze. Now we don't know who the dead man is. Of course I'm worried."

Eileen rolled her eyes. "I meant about Wolfe. Your relationship. I know you, and I know that expression. Are you having doubts?"

Faith thought for a moment about how truthful to be with her aunt. "I suppose they're more like insecurities. I mean, I've caught Lighthouse Bay's most eligible bachelor. He wines and dines me as if I'm some kind of heiress." She motioned to their impressive surroundings. "I can't help but feel a bit out of my league."

"Nonsense," Eileen chided. "Trust me, if a man like Wolfe is working that hard to sweep you off your feet, then he means it. Wolfe knows what a treasure you are, just like Brooke, Midge, and I do."

Eileen had named Faith's closest friends in Lighthouse Bay and the other two members of the Candle House Book Club. Faith couldn't imagine life without such warm and loyal companionship. The adventures they had together were the real treasures.

"Maybe our mystery needs a spot on the club agenda tomorrow," Faith suggested, suddenly wanting to move the subject away from her relationship. "It couldn't hurt to have you, Brooke, and Midge putting your minds together on the puzzle of Red's apparent double."

"Great idea," Eileen agreed. "We'll probably have a dozen theories cooked up by the time our meeting's over." She winked. "If you're not too tired from another date with your handsome bachelor."

"We do have a date tonight, but you know I'd never miss a meeting of the book club. Actually, I thought we'd have to cancel our dinner at The Blue Fin, but we're still on."

"Very elegant," Eileen teased. "Wine and dine indeed. I've always wanted to go there."

"I'll be sure to give you a full report."

Eileen glanced up as one of the groundskeepers guided a sleek black convertible across the lawn. "Wow, that one's impressive."

They watched as a gorgeous Porsche roadster rolled onto the grass to take its place next to the convertible.

Eileen grinned. "Spies do love their fancy cars."

"Says the woman who traded in her basic sedan for a snazzy red convertible," Faith replied. She adored Eileen's zest for life. It was one of the best things about her aunt.

"Can't you picture Trey Connor getting out of any one of those?" Eileen pointed to the growing selection of posh, spy-worthy vehicles that were being lined up on the grass. "I don't think he'd bother with my little Mustang."

Faith nudged her aunt. "Now who's downplaying herself? I love your Mustang. It's perfect for you. These cars look so expensive I'd be afraid to get behind the wheel."

The back of a silver trailer opened up to reveal a silver vintage convertible. Two men slowly and carefully maneuvered the car out onto the grass.

"Now that's something I don't understand," Eileen said. "What fun is a fancy car if you don't actually drive it?"

"I don't know," Faith answered. "Wolfe drives his fancy cars all the time."

"Are you taking one of his cars up the coast tonight? The weather is going to be perfect for a long drive along the water."

"I doubt we could show up at The Blue Fin in my SUV," Faith said. She glanced at the lawn again and noticed Wolfe shaking hands with the owner of the first sports car. She thought he seemed right at home among the luxurious vehicles she'd just declared herself too afraid to drive.

"Did I hear you say models were coming in for this too?" Eileen asked.

A lingering pinch of doubt tightened in Faith's chest. "Yes. The women who have appeared on some of the previous Trey Connor book covers are competing to be featured on the final cover."

"So, impressive curves of more than one kind, hmm?" Eileen squinted at her knitting, redid a stitch, and continued.

One car gunned its engine as it moved into place.

The sound woke Watson. After a moment's consideration, he returned to his nap, evidently unimpressed with the mechanized purrs going on in front of him.

"Ten models," Faith said with no enthusiasm. "It feels like we're hosting a beauty pageant on top of a book event and a car show."

She'd never admit it to Eileen, but Faith's lack of sleep made her feel worn-out and frumpy. It definitely wasn't helping that by this time tomorrow she'd be surrounded by stunning women.

Faith sighed. "I can't help but remember that Wolfe was engaged to a model once."

Eileen stopped knitting. "Stop that. History is just that—history. Wolfe has eyes only for you. You work in an amazing setting with exciting things happening all around you. Enjoy it."

"I do," Faith said. "At least I think I would if I were sleeping better. I'm so tired that it's making me cranky."

"It sounds like what you need is a nice evening out with a dashing man." Eileen smiled. "Good thing that happens to be on your agenda."

"What's also on my agenda," Faith said as she rose from the chair, making Watson jump from her lap with a grumble and scamper toward the library, "is a long list of reference requests. I did love our break, but I really should get back to work."

Eileen packed up her knitting, then stood and gave her niece a tight hug. "You return to your library, and I'll return to mine." Eileen was the librarian at the Candle House Library in Lighthouse Bay. "By the way, I peeked at our choice for tomorrow night's read. *The Blood of Sisters* is going to be intriguing."

"Good," Faith said. "I could use the distraction."

The bustle of guests arriving at the manor could be so tiresome. The cat found today especially unamusing. The library windowsill was one of his favorite places for an afternoon nap. Sunshine bathed the sill today as always, but the quiet he preferred was nowhere to be found. Instead, the ruckus from the terrace right outside made a decent nap impossible.

And the dogs. All that running and barking and snuffling and slobbering. The cat had always thought spies were to be admired—sleek stealth and cunning plans being very catlike qualities—but these people weren't spies. They only liked reading about them from the loud man with red hair who had a very excitable dog.

Only this man was confusing. The cat could not quite work out how he had miraculously recovered from his deathlike state in the manor shrubbery. He'd become an astute student of human behavior, and he was relatively certain even loud men did not recover from the state he'd seen the red-haired man in underneath the boxwood bushes. Which could only mean there had to be two red-haired men. Something was unusual about that, and he aimed to find out exactly what it was.

"Hello there!" The red-haired man tapped on the window from the outside.

Seconds later the large black nose of the dog pressed up against the window as well.

That was the thing about dogs. They left nose prints everywhere as they pushed their way into spaces before they were invited.

When the red-haired man peered in and waved to his human, the cat jumped from the sill and dashed up to the second-floor balcony.

"Hello again, Miss Newberry," the man called as he opened the library door less than a minute later.

The cat was pleased that the human wasn't so bold as to bring the dog with him into the library.

His human stood. "Please call me Faith. I'm so sorry about everything that's happened, Mr. Maxton."

At the mention of the day's earlier events, the man's face flashed a moment of anxiety. "Please call me Red," he replied. "And let's not talk of that."

The cat's whiskers twitched. The man was trying to look happy, but any cat with a decent intuition could see he was really very frightened. It didn't take any espionage to figure that out. Was this red-haired man afraid he would end up like the other red-haired man?

"Why don't you join us out on the terrace?" the man asked.

His human made polite objections that she had important work to do, but she finally relented and allowed the man to usher her out to the terrace.

The cat ran out of the library and dashed upstairs to the second floor. A peek in the man's room might tell him what was going on. The cat entered one of the secret passageways and trotted down it. He exited the closet in the dark-paneled bedroom where the man was staying.

He was unsurprised to discover that the man's room was a mess of tossed clothing and scattered papers. Loud humans were often untidy creatures.

He walked past the ridiculous amount of dog toys, poking instead through the disarray. His whiskers tingled in attention to every detail, alert for a clue he could not yet identify but was sure would be here. Clues were always there, if a clever cat knew where to search.

The clue was not in the closet where clothes hung half off their hangers. It was not in the pile of towels in the bathroom, nor in the two open suitcases sitting beside the bed.

The cat kept searching. He knew there was something to learn in this room.

There it was. The open briefcase tossed beside the desk held a sight that made the cat stop and stare.

Clipped to a stack of typed pages filled with angry red marks was a photograph. An older photograph, like the kind his human kept in her research files. A shiny black-and-white square with a white border and a grainy image inside it.

This explained a lot about the mystery of the red-haired men and why he was so upset.

His human needed to see this. The cat would just have to figure out how to show it to her.

Book club gatherings were always a highlight of Faith's social calendar. The warm conversation among friends and interesting reads suggested by the members always made for a memorable time.

Tired as she was, Faith still smiled as she and Watson entered the Candle House Library Saturday morning.

She could have sworn a similar smile appeared on the face of the energetic little Chihuahua who waddled into the room ahead of Midge Foster a few minutes later. Atticus was a friendly dog, often sporting adorable outfits and his Doggles, specially outfitted dog glasses to correct his vision problem. Atticus was as much a fixture at book club meetings as Watson.

"Hello, Atticus," Faith said.

Atticus returned her greeting with a yip.

"Sorry I'm late," Midge said with a frustrated sigh. "The oven was giving me trouble with the last batch of tunaroons, and I knew someone would never forgive me if I arrived without them." The vet shook a small bag in front of Watson.

The cat immediately perked up at the sight of his favorite treat.

"Five minutes isn't late in my book," Brooke said. "Especially when a finicky oven is to blame. There were days I was ready to take a sledgehammer to the ovens at the manor before we upgraded last spring."

"I'm thinking an upgrade—or at least a replacement—is in my future," Midge said. "A veterinary practice is all the uncertainty I need in life. My baking should be thoroughly predictable." In addition to serving as the concierge veterinarian for Castleton Manor, Midge owned the Happy Tails Gourmet Bakery in town. "But I hear it's the gardens serving up surprises this week," she remarked to Faith as she slid into one of the chairs.

"A body in the hedge maze, to be exact," Eileen said as she passed out cinnamon scones and cups of coffee.

"One that's a dead ringer—pun intended—for our guest of honor," Faith added. "It was quite a shock when Red Maxton walked onto the grounds alive and well."

"So who is the man in the hedge maze?" Midge asked as Atticus curled up in her lap.

"Other than someone who looks exactly like Red Maxton, we don't know," Faith said. She took a sip of coffee. "There was no identification on the body."

"Does Red have any idea?" Midge asked.

"He doesn't seem to, and he's legitimately upset," Faith replied. "He thinks whoever murdered the man in the hedge was out to murder him."

"That would definitely scare me," Brooke said, then took a bite of her scone.

"He acts as if everything is fine for the attendees, but he hardly talks to anyone and mostly stays in his room," Faith said. "When he's not asking Wolfe about how the security's been beefed up, that is."

"Famous people have different problems than we do." Brooke shook her head. "Dead doubles. It sounds crazy."

"It's sad and tragic. And creepy. I don't blame Red for refusing to view the body." Faith shuddered. "I'm not sure I'd want to view a murdered victim who looked like me either."

"Could it be somebody's idea of a retirement party joke? I mean, before he was murdered," Midge said. "Or maybe a misguided fan dressing up like his favorite author?"

"Whatever it is, it's gruesome," Eileen said with a frown. "So Red thinks someone was trying to kill him?"

"Or at least send the message that he could be next," Brooke chimed in. "It seems like a long way to go for something that could be written in a note. And it's much more extreme than a prank. Besides, it's not as if Red is actually a spy. He only writes about fictional ones."

"Maybe he really is a spy," Midge said with a dramatic flair.

"I doubt that," Eileen said as she removed her latest knitting project from her tote and set to work. "But it's got to be important that the victim could be a clone of Red."

Faith nodded. "Now we need to figure out why."

The Candle House Book Club had a long history of solving mysteries together. In fact, Faith would wager they spent as much time solving mysteries as they did socializing and discussing books. With these good friends at her side, life was never boring nor any puzzles unsolvable.

"If it's not about Red himself, what if it has something to do with his retirement?" Midge posed. "After all, the killer chose his celebration to commit the murder."

"I'm not sure how that could be a motive," Brooke commented. "But it could be opportunity. Think about it. Where else would you be more likely to find a Red Maxton double than at a Red Maxton gathering?"

"If you follow that line of thinking, the murder could have nothing to do with Red and everything to do with the look-alike," Midge said.

"We shouldn't go too far with that theory until we know who the victim was," Eileen advised.

"We don't know anything on that front yet," Faith said. "Garris told me he's running the man's fingerprints, but unless he's got a criminal record or had to get a security clearance of some kind, that may not help."

"It's not as if Garris can pass around a photo or put out a bulletin asking if anyone knows the man," Brooke said. "Everyone would say it's Red Maxton."

Midge thought for a moment. "Rather a brilliant way to hide your victim, isn't it?"

"I hadn't thought of it that way," Faith replied. "But you're right. A doppelgänger for a live celebrity is a clever way to make your victim unidentifiable."

Brooke pointed at Faith. "Especially if you know that celebrity will be close by. Wow, this is starting to sound more and more worthy of a Trey Connor novel all the time."

"Now I'm almost sorry we didn't pick one of Red's books to read this month," Eileen said. "Reading one of them might help us solve this murder." She picked up the stack of *The Blood of Sisters*.

Brooke took a book from Eileen, grimacing at the gruesome image on the cover. "I doubt that. We're in little old Lighthouse Bay, and Trey Connor's adventures are about cutting-edge gadgets and far-flung places. I let Diva and Bling watch the movie set in the Amazon with me since angelfish are from there."

Brooke often treated her fish to experiences far beyond most pets. The chef felt Diva and Bling were extraordinary for their species. Usually the "emotions" of her angelfish reflected what Brooke was feeling herself. However, given Faith's beliefs about Watson's extraordinary skills and perception, how could she argue with Brooke's view?

Eileen passed a copy of *The Blood of Sisters* to Faith. "Brooke's right. Spy gadgets and evil geniuses aren't likely to help us find out what happened to the victim under the hedge maze. But what about the gun's registration?"

"It doesn't seem to have one, at least that I've heard," Faith answered. She scanned the book jacket of the thick hardcover. "What's this one about again?"

"It's a mystery about forensic science," Midge explained. "The sleuth is a chemist on a high-level government project. She finds the killer using DNA. My friend said it's fascinating."

"I need fascinating," Faith said. "And not a spy book. I think I'll have more than my fill of espionage by the time this event is over. The cars are nice to look at, but the models are difficult."

"They've arrived, have they? A competition to be on the last book cover sounds more dramatic than exciting to me." Midge made a face. "I imagine things could get a bit tense in that setting."

"You can say that again." Brooke rolled her eyes. "These women have been rude, and they make snide comments about everything, including the food."

"If it's this bad before the model competition even starts this afternoon, I'm worried things will get out of hand," Faith said.

"*Get* out of hand?" Brooke put her hand to her forehead. "We've already found a dead body we thought was our guest of honor in the hedge maze. This week was out of hand before it even started."

"I'm almost afraid to ask, but what's this afternoon?" Midge said.

"An evening gown competition." Faith tried not to let her distaste for the event show. The manor had hosted a number of eccentric functions, and she tried to never let her approval or disdain taint how she performed her professional duties.

"It sounds like a beauty pageant," Midge said.

That's what I thought, Faith agreed silently. "Red, his editor, and the audience get to choose the winner to be on the book cover."

"Then it's definitely a beauty pageant," Midge said. "I remember our Miss Frog Eye pageant when I was growing up in Alabama. There was a lot of sinister hiding behind some of those gleaming smiles."

"Some of the models have been nice," Faith felt compelled to say.

In fact, a few of the beauties had been especially friendly to her. Of course, they'd been especially friendly to Wolfe as well. Not that she was noticing. Faith had always been comfortable with her appearance, but walking through a hallway of gorgeous models could make any woman resurrect her insecurities.

"I'd rather talk to a woman with a brain and a backbone over one in a bikini any day," Eileen said. "So I'm going to enjoy reading about our crime-solving chemist with all my smart and strong woman friends."

Faith couldn't agree more.

"Some parts of this job are going to be harder to leave behind than others," Red announced with a dramatic air as he regarded the collection of beautiful women surrounding him onstage.

Faith, Wolfe, and Red's editor, Nick Westfield, stood in the back of the banquet hall. A stage had been set up on one end of a long, raised walkway that ran down the center of the room with chairs on either side. The setup resembled that of a pageant or a fashion show.

Nick grinned. "Red's playing this for all it's worth. But can you blame the guy? Ten cover models to choose from, and Red can—" He squinted at the stage. "Hey, wait a minute. We're missing one."

"What?" Faith asked.

"There should be ten women up there. I only see nine." Nick glanced around. "Where's Olivia Bishop?"

Marlene hurried over to the little group. "We have a situation upstairs with Ms. Bishop." She turned to Wolfe. "Could I see you for a moment, please?"

To anyone who didn't know Marlene well, the woman would have seemed calm and collected, but Faith could see that she was anything but.

"I should come," Nick offered.

"No, you stay here and see to the competition and the attendees," Wolfe said. "I'll check on Ms. Bishop and send her down when we've taken care of whatever the problem is."

Faith followed Wolfe out into the hallway, not about to miss whatever news Marlene had to convey.

"Ms. Bishop's suite was broken into," Marlene said. "And her evening gown was slashed."

Faith gasped.

"Is she all right?" Wolfe asked.

"Of course not," Marlene said as she began leading them up to the second floor, where the guest rooms were located. "The woman's hysterical."

"I can understand that," Wolfe said. "But is she unharmed?"

"Physically," Marlene answered. "Her room was ransacked while she was in the shower. The person destroyed her gown and put it back in the closet so she wouldn't see the damage until it was too late."

"Obviously, someone wanted her out of the competition," Wolfe said as they reached the second-floor landing.

Marlene stopped outside the Daphne du Maurier Suite. With a cautious glance at Faith and Wolfe, she knocked on the door. "Ms. Bishop, I have Mr. Jaxon, co-owner of the manor, and Miss Newberry, the librarian, with me. May we come in?"

The door opened to reveal a graceful woman with her hair and makeup flawlessly done, but she was clothed in a turquoise silk robe. Olivia Bishop appeared to be closer to Red's age than the other models, so Faith guessed the woman was among the first of the Connor cover models. She may have had a few years on some of her competition, but she was still a stunning woman.

"Gracious, I can hardly believe it!" Olivia cried in a strong Southern accent as she let the three of them into the room. "I knew things would be tense here, but this is downright vicious."

Faith's attention was immediately drawn to the sparkly red dress spread out on the bed and slashed in several places down the front. Sequins littered the bedspread and carpet like blood from a wound. "I'm so sorry this happened to you," Faith said.

"The expense is bad enough, but to think someone wanted me out of the competition this badly . . ." Olivia put a hand over her mouth to stifle a sob. "I don't understand it."

Wolfe offered Olivia his hand. "I'm Wolfe Jaxon, and I'll try to do whatever I can to assist you."

"Olivia Bishop," she said as she shook his hand. "Thank you."

"Has anything other than your dress been damaged?" Faith asked.

"Other than my chance to be the first and last Trey Connor cover model?" Olivia asked.

"You have every reason to be upset," Wolfe said. "This is a disturbing situation, but we need your help to remedy it. Do you know if your dress is the only thing that's been damaged?"

Olivia seemed to soften a bit at Wolfe's calm voice. "Yes. Well, at least I think so. I haven't really checked."

Faith began a slow circle of the room, searching for anything that seemed out of place. There were several rounds to this competition, so it was feasible that whoever did this could have damaged more of Olivia's possessions.

"Oh, my bracelets!" Olivia exclaimed. She rushed over to a bureau and opened a makeup case. After removing a red velvet pouch from the case, she withdrew a set of rhinestone cuff bracelets and held them up. "Thank goodness. I wore these on the first Trey Connor cover."

Faith studied the rows upon rows of sparkling rhinestones set atop gold mesh. "They're beautiful."

Olivia put the bracelets away. Then she went over to a violin case and carefully took out the instrument. "This appears to be fine too," she said, relief clear on her face as she examined it.

Faith walked over to the closet. "Do you mind if I peek in here?" she asked, not wanting to add snooping to the list of Olivia's current grievances.

Olivia returned the violin to its case. "Go ahead."

Faith opened the closet and poked around the clothing on hangers and inside the open suitcase. She didn't see any damage to the other clothes.

Olivia dabbed her eyes with a tissue and swayed a bit.

Wolfe pulled out the chair from the desk. "Please sit down and tell me what you know."

Olivia collapsed into the chair. "I was in the shower and later in front of the bathroom mirror doing my hair and makeup. I'm pretty sure I had the door locked, but I can't say for certain. I didn't hear anything. Then again, with the shower and then the blow-dryer running, how would I?"

Wolfe nodded.

"I didn't notice the dress at first because it was still in the closet," Olivia explained. "It wasn't until I took it out that I saw what had happened."

Faith moved her search for clues to the nightstand and the bed.

"And then what happened?" Wolfe asked.

"Well, I screamed and threw it on the bed. Not that anyone heard me, since they were all downstairs." Olivia crossed her arms over her chest. "Red and Nick are going to love this."

"Surely they'll be upset," Faith said, curious about Olivia's odd answer.

"Don't be so certain," Olivia replied. "I've known those two for a long time. They love drama, and this definitely qualifies. Red might feel badly, but Nick is likely to make an even bigger deal out of the whole thing for publicity."

"I can't believe that," Marlene said.

"Why do you think I'm not downstairs shouting accusations?" Olivia asked. "I'm in no hurry to play into that hand."

"Speaking of playing into hands," Faith said, pointing to what she'd just discovered.

"My word!" Olivia yelped.

A three of diamonds playing card was stuck to Olivia's bed pillow. A large pin had been stabbed through the center diamond, as if the pillow were a voodoo doll.

5

"I think our problem is bigger than Red Maxton," Wolfe said.

Olivia stared at the playing card pinned to her pillow. "Nothing's bigger than Red Maxton. But that doesn't matter. Please get that thing out of my room immediately."

Thinking quickly, Faith took the plastic bag from the unused ice bucket in Olivia's room and carefully used it to pull the pin from the pillow, remove the card, and tuck both into the bag. "Chief Garris will want these as evidence. I think we have to assume someone is trying to undermine the whole affair, not simply scare Red."

Olivia scooped up the damaged dress and tossed it unceremoniously onto the floor of her closet. "Nick would get a kick out of that."

"Why would he want his own event ruined after all the work he put into it?" Marlene asked.

Olivia's lips tightened into a thin line, as if she'd said more than she planned. She paused, then waved the inquiry away. "Let's just say I wouldn't put anything past Nick Westfield. After all, I need the man to like me if I have any hope of winning this contest after missing the first round."

Faith and Wolfe exchanged glances, and Faith could tell he was as confused and concerned by the model's comments as she was.

"I'll send someone up to change the linens," Marlene said, taking charge of logistics. "I'm sure that will help you feel better. And I'll have tea brought to your room."

"That's kind of you." Olivia dabbed at her face with a tissue. "Now if you don't mind, I'd prefer some privacy to get my wits about me again."

"Of course," Wolfe replied. "I'll instruct the housekeeping staff to keep a close eye on things. If there's anything we can do to make you more comfortable, please don't hesitate to ask."

"Thank you," Olivia said.

They took their leave.

"You don't really believe Nick could be behind this, do you?" Faith whispered as they walked down the hall.

Wolfe frowned. "It seems unlikely. We reached him in New York only hours after we found the body."

"Except that we called the number he gave me, which was his cell," Marlene interjected. "So he could have been anywhere."

"Including Lighthouse Bay," Faith added gravely. "Perhaps we'd better keep a closer watch on Nick Westfield."

The evening gown round of the model competition went on without Olivia, but the story of what had happened to her dress spread quickly among the guests. Marlene, Wolfe, and the rest of the staff attempted to keep news of the body discovered in the hedge maze in the background, but everyone knew that it was a losing battle.

By the time Faith, accompanied by Watson, arrived at the library to get in a little peaceful cataloging after Sunday services the next morning, it was clear tensions around the manor had risen considerably. She might catalog, but it stood little chance of being peaceful.

She chose instead to hide away in the back of the library's ornate second-floor balcony, cleaning shelves and checking bindings. At least that offered a few hours of solitude until the door opened below her in the early afternoon.

"No one is out to kill you," Nick snapped. "Get ahold of yourself. You can't let people see you like this."

Faith leaned toward the railing to see Red and Nick embroiled in what sounded like a heated conversation. They'd stepped into the library, apparently assuming they were alone.

"How can you be so sure?" Red asked. "I'm telling you, whoever shot that man in the hedge thought he was shooting me. What's to stop him from coming back to finish the job when he learns he merely shot a decoy?"

"How do you know it's a 'he'?" Nick asked. "Given your history, it could easily be a 'she.' Don't forget Olivia's here. She's always been a dramatic mess."

"I know exactly what Olivia is like and what she's capable of." Red stared at Nick. "Do you?"

Faith glanced across the room from her high vantage point and saw Watson in his customary place on the windowsill. She waved slightly, trying to catch the cat's attention. If she could somehow coax the cat into interrupting the arguing pair, she wouldn't have to announce her presence or admit what she'd already heard.

Watson, however, continued to sit on the sill and stare out the window as if ignoring the intruders would make them go away.

Nick leaned casually against the side of the library's large carved fireplace mantel. "Come on. I've taken care of Olivia before, and I can do it again. Don't let your history mess you up here."

Red grunted as he tossed a leather briefcase onto one of the plush red upholstered chairs that faced the fireplace. "That's all in the past. It has nothing to do with what's happening right now."

"Her dress was shredded, and there was a three of diamonds on her pillow," Nick reminded him. "You have to admit that's a nasty thing to do."

"What did you expect?" Red bellowed. "You've turned my retirement party into a beauty pageant. Did you really think those models were going to play nice when you dangled a big cover contract in front of them?"

"I don't get it. You used to love this sort of stuff." Frustration began to creep into the editor's tone.

"That was before someone tried to kill me." Red ran his hands down his face. "I didn't even want this party. You know I didn't."

Faith cleared her throat softly in an attempt to signal her presence, but the men were so engrossed in their argument that they failed to hear her.

"Why can't we release the final book and let that be it?" Red went on. "I'm exhausted. Besides, I've made enough money off Trey, and so have you."

Nick gave a sour laugh. "Because I know you. You don't really want to quit. You only think you do. Go on and admit it."

"Is that why you did all of this?" Red gestured toward the lawn, where the sports cars were parked on display.

His raised voice and the sweep of his hand caught Watson's attention, and the cat glared at the men.

"Did you bring these models, cars, and fans here to try to dazzle me into changing my mind?" Red went on.

Nick shifted his weight. "Listen, the last two movies did exceptionally well. You've got momentum going in your favor. The movie studio wants three more movies. That means three more books. Do you honestly want me to reject their generous offer?"

Red jabbed a finger at Nick. "As a matter of fact, I do. Tell them no. I own Trey. He's my creation. If I say I'm done, then I'm done."

Nick crossed his arms over his chest and regarded Red with a smug expression. "You should read your contracts more carefully."

Faith gulped. The gloves were coming off now.

"What are you talking about?" Red demanded.

"If you checked your contracts, you'd know that the publisher owns Trey," Nick stated.

"There's no way. My name is on all the book copyrights."

"You may own those copyrights, but legally, we own the characters. We license the movies, not you." After what was clearly meant to be an intimidating pause, Nick said, "Which means that technically I could say yes to the studio. Without you."

Red widened his stance, and Faith thought he might actually charge Nick. "With what story?" Red asked, his voice lowering to a growl. "You wouldn't dare."

"So don't make me," Nick responded. "Screenwriters are a dime a dozen, but I don't want to go that route. Come on. Give me three more books. You could knock off that many in your sleep. They don't even have to be great."

"What's that supposed to mean?" Red roared. "Are you telling me you think anyone could do what I do? Is that actually what you're saying?"

Faith had already overheard too much. She stepped out of sight toward the rear of the balcony and knocked a book off the shelf. "Oh, how clumsy of me," she said loudly enough that she knew the two men would hear.

"What on earth?" Red asked.

"Hello?" she called as innocently as she could manage. "Is someone there?" She came to the railing, trying to feign surprise. "I thought I heard voices. Good afternoon, gentlemen. I'll be right down."

The two men were silent.

Faith descended the small spiral staircase that connected the second-floor balcony to the rest of the grand library.

Watson leaped off his spot on the windowsill to nonchalantly stroll between the two men.

"Hello there," Red said as he leaned down to meet Watson's upturned face. "You're quite the library cat, aren't you?" His harsh tone was gone, though Faith thought she could still see remnants of fury in his eyes.

Faith was glad that her cat was doing his part to keep the peace—finally. She felt it would help everyone save face if she continued to behave as though she hadn't overheard their heated exchange. "Yes," she replied brightly, "Watson's a fixture at the manor. And he comes with his own tuxedo," she joked, nodding toward

Watson's black-and-white coat. "Something I imagine Trey Connor might endorse."

"I have to say, the manor's pet-friendly policies are a great amenity," Nick chimed in with the same obvious relief at something safer to discuss than author-editor tensions. "We have no cats among our party, but many of the guests were delighted their dogs could come and hang out with the legendary Rufus."

"What about you, fella?" Red said, running one hand down Watson's sleek back. "You don't mind all these dogs wandering around?"

Watson leaned into the pet, purring loudly.

"Watson has accustomed himself quite well to a wide variety of pets who visit the manor," Faith said. "But I think he considers the library his personal domain."

As if proving her point, Watson jumped onto her desk and sat down right in the middle of it, regardless of the papers she had stacked there neatly.

"I respect a cat who knows when he has to stake a claim to his territory," Red said with a dark look at Nick.

The editor ignored Red's comment and turned to Faith. "Any more news on that unfortunate man in the hedge?"

Red rolled his eyes. "Do we have to bring that up again?"

"I haven't heard any news," Faith said. "But I'm sure Chief Garris will let us know as soon as there are any developments."

"The whole thing is horrifying," Red commented.

"I know we have our differences, but I aged a decade in those hours I believed you were gone," Nick said. His expression softened from their earlier argument, showing real affection for his author. "When I thought it was you they'd found."

It was obvious that fact made Red uncomfortable. "I never thought I'd have the chance to misquote Twain. But I'm glad to say, 'The reports of my death are greatly exaggerated.'"

"So neither of you has any idea who that man is?" Faith asked.

"He's not an overzealous fan or an impersonator you hired in the past?"

"I don't have fans like that," Red said with a prickly tone. "I don't want fans like that."

"I have no idea who he is," Nick answered. "But based on the photo I saw, the resemblance to Red is uncanny. I wish we'd known about him before this."

Faith was taken aback by the callous remark.

Red seemed to agree with her. "Why?" the author challenged. "Were you thinking I needed a stand-in?"

"Don't be so sensitive," Nick chided. "I can't believe you don't find it the least bit intriguing. Doesn't everyone want to meet their double?"

Not that way, Faith thought. "I think I'd be kind of spooked," she admitted. "Especially if that double wound up dead at my party."

Red didn't say anything. He merely glared at Nick.

"Be reasonable," Nick said. "You can't possibly think I'm behind this. I've pulled a lot of stunts, but this goes much further than anything I could ever dream up."

"Forgive me if I'm not convinced," Red muttered.

"So no one has contacted you about acting as your impersonator or anything like that?" Faith asked Red.

The author sat down hard on one of the red chairs. "I don't know who the man is, why he was here, or what anyone wanted with him. I don't want to know. I don't want anything to do with it. Just let the police find out who did it so I can get through this party Nick's shoving down my throat."

"As far as you know, does the incident have anything to do with the event?" Faith asked.

"Nothing whatsoever," Red declared. "Unless Nick knows something he's not sharing." The words held the tone of a thinly veiled threat.

"And what about Ms. Bishop's gown?" Faith persisted.

"I'm sure it was one of the younger models going overboard in an effort to grab the final cover," Nick said.

"Well, find out who did it and remove her from the competition,"

Red ordered. "I don't want someone getting my cover by those underhanded means."

"Not that I don't agree with you," Nick said. "But again, it's really not your call."

Red's face flushed. "I've had enough of you telling me where my say begins and ends in this. Watch your tone. You need me more than I need you right about now." He stormed out of the library, slamming the door behind him.

The loud noise made Faith, Nick, and even Watson flinch.

"Temperamental writers," Nick mumbled, shaking his head. "If only I could make books without them."

It wasn't until almost an hour later that Faith discovered Red had left his briefcase in his rush to leave the library.

Actually, she didn't discover it. Watson did. He declared his find by pouncing on the leather satchel and pushing it off the chair. The briefcase opened and spilled its contents out onto the rug, and the cat began pawing at the thick stack of papers.

"Don't damage anything, Rumpy," she chided him.

Watson stopped, his stub of a tail twitching. He obviously didn't appreciate the nickname.

Gathering up the papers, Faith noticed the title page. *The Shadow of Death: A Trey Connor Adventure.* The author was listed as *R. Maxton.* She also noticed the word *terrible* scrawled in angry red ink across the bottom of the page.

"Didn't Red say he was done writing?" Faith asked Watson. "Maybe he was unhappy enough with this manuscript to decide to retire. But it's really none of our business, is it?"

Watson's resulting stare seemed to say, "Everything is my business."

"We need to return this to Red whether you approve or not," Faith said. "Without editorial comment on what's inside."

As Faith slid the stack of papers back into the briefcase, she couldn't help but notice that nearly every page bore harsh comments such as *idiotic*, *clichéd*, and *clumsy*.

Red seemed to be his own worst critic. Not that such an attitude was uncommon among writers. Faith had encountered enough of them to know that brilliant creative minds could often tend toward volatile and self-deprecating moodiness.

Red would likely be mortified that she'd accidentally seen his manuscript and comments, so Faith closed the latch on the case and opted to give it to him with no comment.

After returning the briefcase to Red in his room, Faith ran into Brooke in the hallway.

"Have you started *The Blood of Sisters* yet?" Brooke asked as she walked with Faith to the library.

"I hate to admit it, but I fell asleep halfway through chapter one last night." Faith shrugged. "Who knew a forensic thriller would be the thing to put me to sleep?"

"I guess that's good in your case," Brooke said. "But I wouldn't write the author and tell her."

Faith laughed. "No, I don't think she'd want to hear how grateful I am that I fell asleep reading her novel. I'm amazed I fell asleep at all. The beginning really grabbed my attention. But I am grateful. It was the first good night's sleep I've had in weeks."

"I stayed up too late because I couldn't put the book down," Brooke said. "It's fascinating. You won't believe the things they learn from a single strand of hair."

When they reached the library, Faith unlocked the door, and they went inside.

"This has been a crazy weekend," Brooke remarked. "Did they find out who destroyed Olivia's dress yet?"

Faith shook her head. "Marlene still hasn't worked out how the person got in and out of Olivia's room. You know how she is about keys. Nick thinks it's one model sabotaging another."

"He's probably right. What other motive could there be?"

Faith walked over to the window and gazed out at the semicircle of luxurious cars parked on the lawn. The convertibles were inviting in the June sunshine, and everyone seemed to be crowded around a particular gleaming silver roadster, Wolfe included. "Let's hope the car show will be much less dramatic."

Brooke joined her. "But more expensive," she said with a wry smile. "I heard one of the men at lunch say he owned eleven cars. Can you imagine?"

"Those people travel in a whole different world than we do," Faith said.

Watson jumped up between them.

Did he sense the pinch of self-doubt that plagued her every time she saw Wolfe so at home among the expensive cars and jet-setting models? The way the cat nudged up against her, she could imagine he somehow knew.

Faith reached down to pet her beloved companion. "The only purring engine I'm fond of is the one inside you, Watson."

"But you told us you drove out to The Blue Fin in Wolfe's little blue convertible Friday night. Is it a fun car?"

Faith smiled, remembering their drive down the coast. It had been a lovely evening. They'd zipped alongside the ocean under the stars with a warm breeze flowing over them. "Actually, it is. Wolfe has a great time with it. You can see it in his eyes."

Brooke gave Faith's shoulder a playful bump. "Could be, but if you ask me, that sparkle in his eyes is mostly about you." Her face softened. "Are you two getting serious?"

Faith gave a small sigh. "It's sure starting to feel that way. For me, at least."

"What about for Wolfe?"

"I wish I knew." Faith hugged herself. "He can be so warm and attentive, but he still keeps a wall up around himself. There are times I feel like I know him well and then times when I feel like we're from such different worlds."

Brooke sat down on the broad windowsill next to Watson. "I'll bet it's more about Wolfe being cautious in a new relationship—and with an employee, no less. I've never gotten the sense that he cares much about material objects. The money isn't what makes him. It simply makes lots of things possible for him." She winked. "And maybe for you. Isn't that a good thing?"

"I suppose you're right," Faith said.

Brooke smiled. "Of course I'm right. The chef is always right. It'll work out. Even Diva and Bling are rooting for you."

"I'll try to remember that," Faith replied. Brooke believed her angelfish were excellent judges of romantic prospects, so Faith took the aquatic endorsement as a compliment. She gave her friend a hug. "Thanks."

Brooke pointed to the bright-red coupe that was now barely visible behind an excited knot of people. "What's going on with the last car?"

"I don't know," Faith said as she peered closer.

Wolfe walked away from the group, talking intently on his cell phone. He appeared upset.

Two or three people pointed at the rear tire of the car.

"I think it has a flat tire," Faith said. "But how would it get one?"

"This is getting out of hand, I tell you," Marlene said as she strode into the library. She held up her cell phone as if it were the herald of bad news.

"What is?" Brooke said.

"Wolfe texted me that he's calling Chief Garris about the cars on the lawn," Marlene answered.

"I doubt he's asking for parking or speeding tickets," Brooke said with a laugh. "What's up?"

Marlene frowned, failing to appreciate the joke. "Someone slashed the tires on one of the cars."

"Oh no." Faith turned back to the window to see that all four of the vehicle's tires were flat. Now Wolfe's expression and the commotion around the one car made sense. "The same person who damaged Olivia's dress?"

"Probably," Marlene said. "They found a three of diamonds card tucked under the windshield wiper."

Faith could see the police examining the car as she worked that afternoon, but still no one was any closer to knowing who was playing havoc with Red's retirement festivities.

Watson had left the library some time ago, and she hadn't seen him since. Faith imagined the cat had gone to investigate or take a stroll through the gardens.

She was packing her things to go home when Olivia entered the library with Watson in her arms.

"I wanted to return something I found in my room," Olivia said with a wry smile.

It wasn't unusual for Watson to roam the manor's rooms—even its guest suites—as if he owned the place. But it was unusual for the cat to be carried by a guest and delivered to the library like an overdue book.

"I've been wondering where you've been hiding, Rumpy," Faith said.

"With me," Olivia replied, glancing down at Watson. "He appeared about an hour ago, waltzing into my room as if it was perfectly normal to have a cat suddenly materialize out of your closet."

"I'm so sorry he startled you." Faith frowned at her cat. "I'd like to think he knows better."

"Oh, he did give me a surprise, given everything that happened yesterday," Olivia said. "But I certainly enjoyed his visit. I had two cats for many years. I find them calming company."

Faith kept waiting for Watson to jump down, but he appeared quite content in Olivia's arms. "He seems to like you a lot. That doesn't happen too often with guests."

"I'll take that as a compliment." Olivia sat down in one of the soft upholstered chairs, and Watson settled contentedly in her lap. "I don't mind saying I could use one after all this business."

Faith sat down next to her. "It's a terrible thing about your dress. But I've heard that you're an accomplished violinist, so I'm sure you can make up for it in the talent competition."

"A talent competition," Olivia scoffed. "Can you imagine? I don't agree with how they're running this whole thing like a beauty pageant, and I almost stayed home. It's overdone, but then that's Red and Nick for you. They always go too far."

"It does seem a bit much," Faith said carefully. While Red's party could be considered out of the ordinary, it was far from the strangest event the manor had ever hosted. Some of the themed retreats for booklovers had been highly unusual.

"Though it would be nice to win the spot on the last cover," Olivia said wistfully. "I don't have many more years left in this business."

"That can't be true. You're a beautiful woman by any standards." Faith meant the compliment sincerely. Olivia was a striking woman with a grace many of the younger models simply didn't have. Yes, she'd been dramatic after the ransacking of her room, but wouldn't anyone be under those distressing circumstances?

"Bless your heart," Olivia replied, sounding especially Southern with the phrase. "But I'm afraid modeling is one of those businesses where you can be washed up at thirty." She stroked Watson as she spoke, and Faith could hear him purring.

The cat always seemed to know when Faith needed an extra dose of affection, so she imagined he sensed it in Olivia. She was proud of her pet's compassion.

"That seems unfair," Faith remarked, thankful library science held no such judgment. "A man is considered distinguished as he gets older. Why shouldn't it be the same for a woman?"

"Why indeed? I'm sure most of Red's readers are twice the age of his cover models if not more. Still, I feel fortunate to be working as much as I am. I'd like to go out on a high note if I can."

"As the first and last Connor cover model?" Faith suggested, remembering what Olivia had said when they'd talked in her suite after her dress was damaged.

"Exactly. It would be satisfying to show up those younger women this one time," Olivia said with a wink. "Even if they are willing to go to such nasty lengths to keep me out of the competition."

"So you believe it was one of the other models who slashed your dress?"

Olivia pursed her lips but didn't answer.

"Why do you think the culprit left Trey Connor's calling card?" Faith persisted.

"Drama? Lack of imagination? Publicity?" Olivia pushed out a weary breath. "I don't know, and I'm not sure I really care."

"We found that three of diamonds playing card on the car with the slashed tires this afternoon and on the body in the hedge on Friday. I believe your dress was likely part of a bigger plot to sabotage this whole function."

Olivia raised her eyebrows. "If linking my dress to a murder is supposed to make me feel better, it doesn't."

"Actually I think it should. It means the slashing wasn't against you personally. The culprit was trying to disrupt the event, not take you out of the running."

"It's possible. But then you've got to wonder what else our saboteur has in store." Olivia regarded Watson in her lap. "Better watch your whiskers, Rumpy."

Watson glanced up, then gave a feline glare at Faith. Despite his apparent affinity for Olivia, the idea of his nickname spreading clearly didn't please him.

Best to amend that right away. "That's the nickname I gave him on account of his tail," Faith explained. "I think he prefers Watson, which is his real name."

"Watson," Olivia repeated, angling her face to peer at the cat's green eyes. "I like that. He looks like a Watson. A clever and sophisticated mystery solver, hmm?"

Watson purred, obviously enjoying the praise.

On most days, Faith could be easily convinced that Watson understood far more human speech than anyone gave him credit for.

"There are certainly enough secrets here to keep you busy, Watson," Olivia said.

That remark and Olivia's earlier one tugged on Faith's intuition. "What do you mean by that?"

"Between you and me, I'm not at all surprised that this event has already gone haywire."

Faith raised an eyebrow. "You're not?"

"Given all the expense Nick has gone to for Red, you'd think Nick adored his author, wouldn't you?" Olivia asked.

Faith thought of the exchange she'd overheard earlier. "He doesn't?"

Olivia raised her chin. "Those of us who've been around awhile, those of us with half a brain to see what's going on around them—well, let's just say we know better."

"So things aren't so smooth between Red and Nick."

"I could tell you things about those two that you wouldn't believe," Olivia said. "But I've learned my lesson. I'm keeping my mouth shut."

Faith didn't know how to respond.

Olivia gently nudged Watson off her lap and rose from the chair. "If any of those big secrets are going to come out, you'll have to depend on your Watson to unearth them. And you'd do well to remember he's not the only beast around here with claws."

Faith fought the urge to gulp at the unexpected coldness in the woman's eyes.

"Be sure to keep your eyes peeled at tonight's reception," Olivia said as she walked toward the door. "The next thing to get slashed may not be a dress or a tire but someone's pretty face."

As the door shut behind Olivia, Faith considered the woman's sinister prediction. Olivia felt singled out and clearly wouldn't shy away from giving as good as she got. There was a steely mean streak lurking under all that sweet Southern charm. Was Olivia getting ready to clash with the other models over what had happened to her gown? Or was she planning to pick a fight with Nick or Red?

"Do you want to explain why you've taken such a shine to the likes of her?" Faith asked Watson.

For all his feline intuition, he provided no clue but a twitch of his stumpy tail.

Wolfe offered his arm as he walked with Faith from her cottage toward the glittering reception on the manor's terrace that evening. "It's a perfect night for the party."

"Definitely. Look at that sky."

The heavens were a gorgeous indigo, devoid of any clouds so that every star could be seen. On evenings like this, Faith knew she could walk down to the ocean shore and feel as if she could see forever. Castleton Manor was among the most beautiful places she had ever seen, and it was certainly the most beautiful place she had ever lived. It was easy to understand how the whole Jaxon family loved the estate the way they did and delighted in sharing it with others.

"The sky's not the only lovely thing tonight," Wolfe said with a gleam in his eye.

Faith felt herself blush. "Oh, I agree. The cars are gorgeous too," she teased.

"Very funny," he replied, tucking Faith's hand more tightly into the crook of his elbow. He nodded toward the emerald-green cocktail dress she'd chosen for the reception. "You know, I believe that's my favorite color on you," he said with a warmth that made Faith's skin tingle.

Wolfe was often invited to the more formal parties of Castleton events, and he'd been bringing her along as a friendly companion for some time. Now that he brought her along as a date, Faith felt added stress she wished she could ignore. It was as if being Wolfe's date implied a higher requirement for grace and elegance than being his friend had.

And if that didn't raise the stakes enough, she couldn't help but remember Olivia's sharp warning about tonight's party.

Wolfe gestured to his white dinner jacket. "Men don't get too many color choices in formal wear. Except for teenage proms—or maybe Red Maxton's signature bow tie—we're mostly stuck with black and white."

"Why do you suppose a man named Red insists on wearing a blue bow tie?" Faith mused.

"I think Red does some things simply to be contrary and unexpected. Or maybe the reds clash," he added with a smirk. "You can't be dashing if you're clashing."

Faith moaned at the awful joke. "While your humor leaves a lot to be desired, Trey Connor has nothing on you in the dashing department tonight." It was true. Faith had seen him enough times in both a black tuxedo and a white dinner jacket to know that Wolfe cut a stunningly handsome figure in either one.

Evidently, he'd always been this handsome. Wolfe's mother, Charlotte, had shared a few photos of him as an adorable boy and a swoon-worthy teen. Still, as Faith stared at her date tonight, she had to confirm her earlier remark to Olivia: men did grow distinguished as they matured.

"I hope we don't need Trey's espionage skills tonight. I don't want any more antics marring this event," Wolfe said, glancing at the hedge maze as they passed it.

"Olivia seemed to think the reception wouldn't go smoothly," Faith said. She'd caught Wolfe up on her conversation with the model earlier. "We'll need to be on our toes."

"I asked Garris to keep an eye out around the property tonight." Wolfe shook his head. "I can't believe we still don't know who they found in the hedge."

"It's been two days. How can we not know?" Faith said. "How many people in the world can there be with such an uncanny resemblance to Red Maxton?"

"The chief is every bit as baffled as we are. The only thing he's been able to find out is that the man's hair is naturally red. So it isn't someone dyeing it to try and imitate Red."

"Don't you think they have to be related?" Faith asked. "To have that strong of a resemblance?"

"Garris says no."

"If we had a DNA sample, we could learn for certain if they're related."

"According to Garris, it would take a long time to get the test results," Wolfe answered. "He also thinks he can solve the case without them."

"You'd think maybe Red would want to know if he was related to someone who resembled him that strongly," Faith remarked.

"Maybe you guard your privacy differently when you're a celebrity," Wolfe reasoned.

They reached the steps leading up to the lit terrace, where a jazz combo played and Red's loud laughter could be heard. Faith thought his merriment seemed a little strained.

A waiter glided by with a tray of crystal punch glasses.

Wolfe took two glasses and handed one to Faith. "Let's try to set aside the sleuthing for the moment and concentrate on having a nice evening together."

Faith accepted the drink, complete with a garnish of three strawberry slices cut into diamonds. "Now there's an idea I can get behind."

The rest of the party was a whirlwind of conversations with Red's wealthiest fans. Wolfe talked horsepower and handling with most of the car owners, and Faith was pleased to discover that many of the guests were as fond of books as she was.

The evening bounced between surprisingly comfortable conversations and moments when Faith felt wildly out of place. The people she met vacationed on the French Riviera and owned three homes. And the models spouted on and on about their photo shoots in glamorous locations.

Not to mention how many of the models paid special attention to Wolfe, now that word had gotten out he was unmarried and co-owned the manor.

As one young woman watched Wolfe take Faith's hand, she gave Faith a sneer that said clearly, "I certainly don't consider you any competition."

"Don't pay her shameless flirting any mind," Olivia said, coming up behind Faith at the edge of the terrace as Wolfe stepped away to talk with the owner of the convertible with slashed tires.

"You noticed?" Faith said, glad to know it wasn't just her insecurities playing tricks on her imagination.

"One of the housekeeping staff let it slip that Wolfe was once engaged to a model. Half the women took it as an invitation to zero in on him. But don't you give it another thought. In no time, these models will be out of your hair." Olivia downed her drink. "And mine too, I hope." She fanned herself. "Mercy, but it's hot tonight."

The evening wasn't especially warm, but Faith noticed that Olivia's face appeared flushed.

Olivia put a hand to her forehead and staggered. "Suddenly I don't feel very well."

Faith grabbed her arm to steady her. "Are you all right?"

"I . . ." Olivia glanced down at her glass, and her eyes grew wide. Her breath seemed to come in short bursts. "Land sakes, what's in here?"

Seconds later, she slumped over the terrace wall as the glass of punch slid from her hand to shatter on the tile.

7

Getting Olivia away from the party and up to her room had been a terrible scene. Faith felt herself cringe in sympathy at the unfortunate spectacle Olivia never would have wanted. A visit from the paramedics hadn't helped much. She'd had a violent reaction to something.

Faith and Wolfe watched the ambulance drive away from the manor.

Wolfe shook his head. "Syrup of ipecac in her drink."

The paramedics had confirmed that Olivia had been dosed with the common nausea-inducing drug. Now Chief Garris was collecting the broken glass for analysis.

"I'm glad she didn't need to go to the hospital, but the whole thing is disturbing." Faith had offered to stay with Olivia until she felt better, but the woman had declined, preferring to suffer in solitude.

"It makes you wonder if someone is out to get Olivia, not Red," Wolfe said. "Although I'm not sure how the body in the hedge or the slashed tires would fit into that theory."

Faith sighed. "I don't have any theories at the moment. Except that we'd better solve this murder soon before our culprit strikes again."

Wolfe nodded.

Faith glanced over at Nick, who was doing his best to get the reception back on track. The buzz of alarmed conversation among the guests held no appeal for her, no matter how glittering the party. She faced Wolfe. "If you don't mind, I'd like to go home now."

Wolfe seemed relieved to have an excuse to duck out of the festivities. "I was hoping you'd say that. I've lost my appetite, and I'm definitely not thirsty. I'll walk you to the cottage."

"Thank goodness no one thinks it's food poisoning," Brooke said, relief flooding her features at the news Faith had delivered early Monday morning. She poured two cups of coffee, then joined Faith at the small corner table in the kitchen. "It's terrible that Olivia got sick, but I'm glad to know it couldn't have been my cooking."

Faith accepted one of the cups. "Right before Olivia became ill, she wondered what was in her drink. I don't think anyone ever suspected the food."

"Syrup of ipecac is not very sophisticated, but it's effective." Brooke frowned. "I feel terrible for Olivia. I'd be horrified to be so sick at such an elegant evening. Someone certainly has it out for her."

"They offered to keep her overnight at the hospital for observation, but she insists she's fine. Well, she's angry and queasy but fine."

Brooke took a drink of coffee. "I'll bet Nick feels bad about yelling at her now."

"You saw Nick yelling at Olivia?"

Brooke nodded. "I was in the butler's pantry when they thought the breakfast room was empty yesterday morning."

"What were they arguing about?" Faith asked.

"It was something about the last Trey Connor novel cover."

"I heard Nick and Red arguing in the library when they didn't know I was there," Faith admitted. "Nick doesn't want Red to retire because he has a movie offer coming in. He's trying to get Red to write three more books, but Red doesn't want to."

"Trey Connor is Red's creation." Brooke raised a questioning eyebrow. "I would think he gets to shut the series down if he wants to, wouldn't he?"

Faith sipped her coffee. "You'd think so, but it doesn't sound like it.

Nick was arguing about who owns what and what he can do with or without Red's consent. I have to agree with Red. It doesn't sound like this party is to celebrate Red's retirement. It's to try and convince him to keep writing."

Brooke stood up and began setting out preparations for breakfast. "If that's true, then all these disasters can't help Nick's case. This party's been mayhem from the moment it started. Actually, even before it started."

Faith put down the cup of coffee. "What if that's exactly what he wants?"

"Who?"

"Nick," Faith replied, the connections crackling in her brain. "He's creating an ideal scenario for Trey Connor to swoop in and save the day."

"I don't see how that would help things," Brooke said. "It's not like Trey Connor actually could. He's not real."

"Nick could be trying to make things so exciting that Red will see what he's leaving behind," Faith said. "Look at the events. The beautiful women, the fancy cars, the upcoming gadget exposition—it's everything attractive about Trey's world. And now with danger too."

Brooke set down a stack of serving spoons. "But killing someone? That's going too far, don't you think?"

"Well, that's the part I can't work out," Faith answered. "But there has to be a connection somehow. I stumbled across Red's next manuscript when he left his briefcase in the library. He's clearly not happy with his own work. Maybe Nick's trying to shock him into action again. Get the creative juices flowing."

Brooke placed a handful of serving forks next to the spoons. "If it takes that kind of excitement to write spy novels, I think I'll stick to baking. Like the diamond-shaped shortbread cookies with red frosting for coffee break today."

Faith loved any sweet Brooke created. "They sound delicious. Just make sure nobody keels over after eating them."

Brooke tossed a dish towel at Faith. "Very funny. Those cookies will stay locked up in my kitchen until I personally set them out. I'm leaving nothing to chance with this group."

Faith strolled over to the cars on display during the break, savoring a cup of strong coffee and a couple of scrumptious red diamond shortbread cookies.

After last night's drama, sleep had eluded her again. And while Faith was grateful to get at least halfway through *The Blood of Sisters*, she felt the lack of sleep keenly. With any luck, the coffee, cookies, ocean breeze, and sunshine would provide a much-needed boost to her energy.

As she walked, she recalled Red's earlier presentation. He had discussed the creation of Trey, taking great care to emphasize that the spy was his idea. Whether or not his insistence was for Nick's benefit was anyone's guess.

Faith paused at the first car on the lawn. It was a stately green vintage Jaguar. The sleek, stylized cat seemed ready to leap off the hood.

Nick stood beside the car with his back to her, barking into his cell phone. "I said I'll take care of it, and I will. Everything's under control." He disconnected and stuffed the phone into his pocket.

Before Faith could slip away, Nick turned and saw her. He appeared startled by her presence.

They stared at each other for an awkward moment before Nick picked up a cloth that was sitting on the hood and began buffing the front grille.

"This is yours?" she asked, not sure how else to respond to being caught overhearing yet another of the editor's conversations.

He nodded.

"I didn't realize you were one of the car owners."

"She's not the finest one here, and she wouldn't have a shot at placing in the competition if I'd entered it," Nick said. "But she's precious to me."

Indeed, every owner seemed to treasure their cars, which made the earlier tire slashing that much more despicable.

Faith gestured to the refreshments table set up on the terrace. "You're not with the other guests?" She was surprised Nick was over here by himself, because he didn't seem like one to miss an opportunity to hobnob with Red's fans.

Nick tightened his jaw. "I had to take an important call."

That topic was clearly taboo, so she tried to steer away from it. "What do you especially like about your car?"

"Other than it being tremendously cool and Trey Connor's ride of choice in the third book?" Nick asked, grinning.

"Yes, of course. But there are dozens of other cars that Trey has driven," Faith pointed out. "What made you pick this particular one?"

"For starters, it was the only one in my price range," Nick replied. "I do well for myself, but I'm afraid I haven't yet acquired the deep pockets the rest of these people have."

The deep green of the open convertible and its vintage interior were a treat for the eyes, even in her uninformed opinion. "She is very pretty," Faith commented.

"Her few dings add to her charm for me," Nick admitted. "But you've probably figured out that not every car collector shares my point of view on that."

Faith noticed the car's vanity license plate that read *TREY ED*. "You clearly love the whole Trey Connor mystique."

"I'll be sorry to see it end," Nick said. "If I have my way, it won't."

"I don't know much about publishing," Faith said. "But I do know there are spy and suspense series that have gone on beyond a single author. Would you do that with Trey Connor?"

"Believe me, I'd like nothing better," Nick replied. "However, it can be difficult, especially with someone as touchy as Red. I can do it even without his cooperation. But it gets messy and legally complicated."

"I highly doubt he'd cooperate. Would you take such a drastic step?"

Nick frowned. "Why talk shop when we can talk cars?" The hardness in his eyes told her the subject was officially closed.

Faith had little choice but to follow his lead. "This is a Jaguar, right?" she asked, motioning to the hood ornament.

"The lady knows her sports cars as well as her books. This is an early series. Trey drove Jaguars for the first twelve books. Then Red struck a deal with Lamborghini, and suddenly in the following books, Trey drove one of those." Nick pointed to Red's bright-red Lamborghini that sat in the place of honor in the middle of the semicircle.

It was no surprise that Red's car was an eye-catching red. What other color would the author have?

"That's a nice professional perk," Faith remarked.

"Isn't it? Red's Gallardo is probably the only one in the world that regularly has an Airedale terrier in the passenger seat instead of a supermodel." For as much as Nick claimed to love his own car, his admiration—and perhaps envy—of the more prestigious cars showed in his eyes.

Faith smiled. "I'm trying to imagine Red driving that down the interstate with Rufus's head hanging out the window."

"I've seen it. It draws a lot of stares, but then it's always a good thing when Red gets attention."

"Yours is just as nice in a different way," Faith felt compelled to say. "I think I'd feel much more at home in your car than a showstopper like Red's." In fact, she'd always been grateful that Wolfe's BMW convertible was a dignified dark blue.

"Thanks," Nick said, smiling at the compliment. "But don't tell anyone else that the passenger window doesn't wind up anymore or that she skips third gear like it's hopscotch."

"I suppose I feel the same way about old books. The rips and smudges show their lives, not their damage."

"Exactly." Nick paused before asking, "Would you like to sit in her?"

Given his love for the car and the tension between them, the offer surprised Faith. She smiled. "I'd be honored."

Nick made a show of opening the passenger side door for her.

She slid into the posh seat. It felt a bit like being on a movie set. As the stiff ocean breeze tousled her hair, she could easily imagine the car speeding down a curvy highway in pursuit of a dangerous Trey Connor villain.

"Will I find a ray gun or a martini shaker in the glove box?" Faith teased, playfully tapping the silver button on the dashboard.

"Don't!" Nick shouted, reaching into the car toward the small door.

But it was too late. She hadn't meant to open it, but at her touch, the glove box dropped open. What had to be at least two decks' worth of loose playing cards tumbled out, a handful landing in her lap.

Faith yelped.

As she and Nick collected the cards, the strong wind picked them up and scattered them across the lawn.

Examining the handful in her lap, Faith noticed they weren't a regular deck at all. Every single card was the three of diamonds. And the swirling pattern on the back of the cards matched the one the victim in the hedge had been carrying. It dawned on her that it also matched the card in Olivia's room. Which meant it likely matched the one under the damaged car's windshield wiper Sunday.

Nick studied her. Surely the man had to know how suspicious this appeared. "Marketing," he explained, his voice tight. "I've been having specialized decks made for years."

"Of course," Faith said casually, despite the alarm bells going off in her mind. It was entirely plausible that Nick had a supply of decks that contained only the three of diamonds. It even sounded like something he would dream up.

But a surge of suspicion ran through her as she exited the car.

The feeling only doubled as Faith took a moment to study the other cars on display. She suddenly realized that a three of diamonds had been tucked under the windshield wiper of every single show car.

And every car's tires had been slashed.

"Do you believe Nick?" Wolfe asked.

Red, Nick, and all the Trey Connor event guests were on a sunset cruise that evening, so Faith and Wolfe had taken advantage of the quiet to have a casual dinner together on the small patio at her cottage. They sat at a table with glasses of iced tea and discussed the recent chaos while two steaks cooked on the grill.

"I admit it looks bad for him," Faith answered. "But Garris is right—the evidence is completely circumstantial. It's entirely plausible for him to have a supply of those cards, and no one saw him damaging any of the cars while they were in full view on the lawn."

Wolfe got up and flipped the steaks, their sizzling aroma drawing Watson outside.

The cat sat in a spot of fading sunshine on the stone wall that surrounded the small patio and sniffed the air.

"I'm sorry, but there will be no steak for you," Faith told Watson. "Although there's a couple of tunaroons for you with the individual raspberry cheesecakes I bought from Snickerdoodles for dessert."

"Nick talked his way out of it very slyly," Wolfe continued when he returned to the table. "If Red hadn't defended him, I don't believe the other guests would have let him on the yacht." He glanced in the direction of the coastline. "Then again, Red may be making him walk the plank even as we speak."

Faith laughed. "There's no plank on that ship."

Wolfe winked. "That we know of."

"Do you think Nick did it?" Faith asked. While he appeared guilty, Faith had learned that appearances can often be deceiving. She hadn't yet decided about Nick for herself.

Wolfe thought for a moment. "Nick certainly had opportunity. He was right there, and he had the playing cards in his glove box. I think he's capable of it, but after talking to some of the other car owners, I could say that of several of them."

"Cutthroat competition out there on the lawn?" Faith asked.

"I must admit that those car owners give the models a run for their money. Speaking of which, have you heard the way those young ladies talk about each other?"

"I'm sorry to say I have."

Wolfe shook his head. "All the beauty is on the outside, that's for certain."

A small part of Faith admitted to a guilty pleasure at hearing how Wolfe didn't seem to be taken in by the models' glamour. Eban and several of the other young men on the manor staff were downright starstruck at the parade of models. Faith found it reassuring to know Wolfe didn't count himself among them. However, his indifference didn't seem to stop several of the women from gathering around him at every opportunity.

"Olivia's taken the worst of that, I'm afraid," she said. "Although I'm not convinced it's one of the other models who slashed her dress or tampered with her drink."

"What do you mean?" Wolfe asked.

"She knows something about Red and Nick."

"What does she know?"

"She wouldn't say," Faith replied. "I thought it was rather odd for her to dangle a secret like that in front of me and then not tell me anything else."

"Did she tell you that before or after her misfortunes?" Wolfe asked. "Maybe she wanted you to know why she was a target without betraying Red or Nick."

Faith took a sip of iced tea. "She said it after the dress was slashed but before the reception. And I told you she warned me of something happening that night. I haven't had a chance to ask her about it."

Wolfe raised a dark eyebrow. "I give her credit for still being here."

"I do too. I think I'd go home, given the circumstances. But evidently Olivia doesn't back down so easily."

"They should award the cover to her for sheer mettle alone."

Faith lifted her glass in a toast. "I agree with you there."

Wolfe went over to the grill and checked the steaks. He slid them onto a platter and returned to the table. As he set the platter down, he leaned over and gave Faith a tender kiss. "I know who I'd choose as the Castleton Manor spokesmodel."

"Candlelight?" she teased, naming a favorite mare of Wolfe's from the stables.

"Horses are fine, but I'm partial to the manor librarian."

Watson chose that moment to jump up onto Faith's lap.

"And her cat too," Wolfe said as he took a seat at the table. "But I share my steak with no one."

"No more crime solving for tonight," Faith declared. "Let's enjoy a quiet evening while we have one."

"I'm all for that," Wolfe agreed.

The rest of the evening was spent in enjoyable conversation. This was the Wolfe that Faith was growing to love—not the global business magnate or the sought-after bachelor but the thoughtful man who simply enjoyed spending time with her. She could be just as happy eating a cone with him on the sidewalk in front of the local ice cream parlor as racing down the coast in his convertible. It was the man, not his position in the world, who was coming to hold her heart. Would it be enough?

"I had a wonderful time tonight," he whispered in her ear as they said good night at her door later. "Growing up, I always liked this place when the gardener lived here. Now I enjoy spending time here even more."

"That fond of Watson, are you?" she asked. It was so satisfying to bring a sparkle of amusement to his eyes.

"Oh, he's nice too." With a final, gentle kiss, he turned toward the manor. "Lock that door and get a good night's sleep. Who knows what tomorrow's car gala will bring?"

Faith waved. "I will. See you tomorrow." She locked the door and threw the dead bolt for good measure. As for the pledge to get a good night's sleep, she could only say it was as much on her wish list as his.

Heading to the kettle in the kitchen, Faith called, "How about a nice cup of herbal tea and a few chapters of *The Blood of Sisters*, Rumpy? It put me to sleep last time."

Watson showed his approval by following her to the bedroom and stretching out smack-dab in the middle of the bed while she changed into her pajamas.

She laughed. "You will leave room for me, won't you?"

Within minutes after the water boiled, Faith was nestled comfortably under the covers with both book and cat.

By the time she emptied the mug, her eyelids were beginning to feel heavy.

"Well, what do you know?" She yawned. "This might work as well as last time."

A crash and a thud pulled Faith from a dream about cars racing along the beach waterline, ducking in and out of the waves like seagulls. She felt Watson tense beside her as she struggled to make out shapes in the dim moonlight.

Then she heard another crash and a thud.

It took a second for Faith to recognize the sound of glass breaking. Bolting from her bed, she grabbed her cell phone from the nightstand and the bathrobe from the foot of her bed.

The sound of a third crash and a thud raced down her spine like an electric shock. She ran to the window.

The clouds parted enough to allow her a view of a dark figure fleeing across the lawn toward the manor.

8

The glass on her living room floor sparkled in the moonlight, but Faith found the sight menacing instead of beautiful. The leaded glass windows in her cottage were one of her favorite features in her home, and someone had lobbed three bricks through them. Not only had the glass shattered, but some of the lead framework in the windows now stuck out in bent and twisted shapes as well as in fragments on the floor.

Her composure was in as many shards as the windows. Fear and anger roiled in her stomach and spiked her pulse.

"Are you sure you're all right? No cuts or bruises?" Wolfe asked for the sixth time as they watched Chief Garris deposit the third brick into an evidence bag.

Faith had called Wolfe right after dialing 911, and both Wolfe and Garris had appeared on her doorstep within minutes. She felt terrible for rousing Wolfe out of bed with a crisis twice in the same week. She was suffering from a lack of sleep, and now she was sure he'd share her deficit.

"Yes, I'm all right," Faith answered. "I'm not hurt. But I'm not exactly calm." Every glance she gave toward her damaged front windows sent her stomach churning.

The physical damage was bad enough, but the sight of the three red diamonds painted on each brick took the incident over the top. Whoever was trying to sabotage the Trey Connor event had obviously trained his or her vicious sights on her. But why?

Faith tried to tell herself that she wasn't a specific target. She recited her earlier words to Olivia, reassurances that she was more likely just the recipient of another attempt to ruin Red's retirement celebration. But it wasn't working.

Not long after Garris finished his initial investigation, workers from an emergency service arrived to cover the broken windows.

Faith felt the sound of their hammers pound against her own ribs like the beating of her heart. The slabs of plywood seemed to mar the spaces where her charming windows had been. All the glass might be swept up within the hour, but there was more to restoring this place as home than replacing the vintage windows. How could she feel safe in here again? Would her lingering fear subside before the windows were back in place?

Even before the crew finished their work, Wolfe pulled Faith into the kitchen. He'd been issuing commands from the moment he showed up on her doorstep, breathless from his sprint across the lawn. "It's not safe for you to stay here," he told her.

Faith could only agree. "I'm sure Eileen will let me stay with her."

"I'm sure she would, but I'd rather have you staying at the manor until we get to the bottom of what's going on."

His suggestion made sense at least for tonight. Why wake up Eileen in the middle of the night when there were empty bedrooms on the private floor of the manor? And as much as this residence was one of her favorite perks of being the manor's private librarian, she'd happily trade that privacy for the feeling of protection tonight.

Faith nodded. "Let me pack a few things."

While Wolfe waited, he consulted with the chief.

Faith packed some food for Watson and tossed a few necessities for the night into a small bag, including a pair of pajamas. But she held little hope of getting any more sleep. Her pulse was still hammering with every sound of crunching glass and banging hammer.

Over and over she heard the shocking sounds of windows breaking and the chilling thud of the bricks hitting her floor. The heavy weights had scraped the floors where they had landed. One brick had struck an end table, chipping one of the corners.

As Faith returned to the living room with her packed bag, she felt a fresh wave of tremors. She hated feeling so rattled, but there seemed to be little she could do to stop it.

Wolfe took her hand. "Let's get you out of here." He opened the front door, then waved to Watson. "You too."

Faith glanced at Wolfe with a surge of gratitude as they began the trek across the lawn to the manor. It meant the world to her that Wolfe took her cat's safety into consideration. Truth be told, it wasn't only Watson's safety that she was grateful for. She very much wanted to keep her furry companion close on such a disturbing night.

It was hours before sunrise, and the lawn sat still and dark as she, Wolfe, and Watson made their way toward the lights of the manor. A chill swept over her as they passed the hedge maze, newly reopened to guests after the earlier gruesome find.

Too many disturbing events had followed that first discovery in the hedges, and Faith didn't care for how this mystery seemed to be getting personal. What else could or would befall Red Maxton's farewell party? Or her?

Keeping a firm hold on Wolfe's hand, Faith turned back once more to get a glimpse of the cottage. Her breath caught as the clouds parted to let a patch of eerie moonlight shine down on her house. The large boards covering her former windows resembled giant bandages on a gaping wound, as if the cottage could physically hurt from such harm.

Wolfe's grip tightened as he steered her toward the manor. "You'll be safe, Faith. I'll see to it. Try not to worry."

She could say she'd try, but any promise to stay calm seemed pointless to make under tonight's alarming circumstances.

As they reached the terrace steps, Wolfe asked the question that had been echoing in her head since the incident. "Do you have any idea why someone would pull you into this?"

"Other than to frighten everyone, I can think of only one."

Wolfe stopped, staring at her. "And what's that?"

"Right before I sat in his car, I overheard a conversation Nick was having on his phone. He was telling someone he had everything under control and that he was 'taking care of it.'"

"That sounds suspicious," Wolfe admitted.

"I also asked him whether he'd resort to continuing the series by handing it off to another writer," Faith continued. "I overheard him threatening to do so when he and Red were arguing in the library."

Wolfe opened the door, letting a welcome wash of light play out across the terrace steps. "He'd do that? Red would let him?"

Watson strolled inside with his usual aplomb, and Faith and Wolfe followed him.

"It didn't sound like Red would actually have to agree," Faith replied. "Nick told Red that the publisher owns the rights to his characters and could license them without Red's permission."

"If I were Red, I'd fight that too," Wolfe said. "Trey Connor is his creation, the cornerstone of his career. Why on earth would he let someone else take over his work?"

"Multiple authors aren't uncommon in a long series," Faith said. "In fact, several coauthorships or multiauthored franchises have resulted in best sellers."

"Do you think Nick realized you overheard both conversations?" Wolfe asked.

"The way he was acting, yes, I think so."

"I still don't see what that has to do with tonight."

Faith wasn't entirely sure herself. "Nick reacted strangely when I asked him if he'd get another author to continue Red's series. It was as if I'd uncovered his secret spy plan or something."

"Maybe that is Nick's plan, and he doesn't want anyone else to know about it," Wolfe suggested. "Now he thinks you've stumbled upon it."

"Why would it matter what I know? Nick has already told Red he's capable of extending the series without Red's consent."

"If you have enough money and lawyers, there's usually a way to do anything. And the more lucrative the deal, the more some people are willing to stretch the bounds of what's right. Or possible. So if Nick thinks you somehow stand in the way—"

"But what I asked isn't a secret," Faith interjected. "What's the point of trying to scare me into silence? It makes no sense. Anyone could come to the same conclusions I did. And since we found all those playing cards hidden in his glove box, everyone's suspicious of him, not just me."

She was glad to feel Wolfe's arm tighten around her shoulders as they mounted the second flight of stairs. It might have been June on the calendar, but tonight's breeze had whirled dark and cold around her.

"I think you're too close to this," Wolfe told her sternly. "I don't like it. Not at all."

"Nick's a professional. Someone of his stature wouldn't stoop to throwing bricks through a window, would he?"

"Anyone can be pushed to unreasonable actions if they feel threatened. You were the one to discover his cache of cards, and you were witness to his being alone with all the show cars right before you noticed the tires were slashed. He could have done it when no one else was around. If he thinks you're onto his plan to destroy the event and replace Red, then maybe he did it to frighten you into keeping quiet."

"If Nick is the one leaving the cards, did he mess with Olivia's drink as well? Slash her dress?" Faith asked. "Don't forget that Olivia told me she knew secrets about Nick and Red."

Wolfe's eyes darkened. "I don't like Nick. At this point, I wouldn't put anything past him."

The strong condemnation surprised Faith. Wolfe was normally the kind of man to give people the benefit of the doubt. "Including murder?"

After a moment, Wolfe said, "I wouldn't rule it out." He stopped on the third-floor landing, seeming to make a decision. "This has gone far enough. We're going to his room right now."

Faith stared at him. "Now? Are you sure you want to confront him without Garris?"

Wolfe nodded. "He's a guest in my establishment, and I have reason to believe he's threatening a member of my staff." He marched back down the stairway.

Faith had never seen Wolfe so worked up. She started down the stairs after him, Watson darting along beside her. "You don't have any proof."

"If Nick is wide-awake or not in his room, then that's proof enough for me," Wolfe said. "I'll call Garris and convince him to take Nick in."

Faith grabbed his arm as she caught up to him. "I'm not sure you can. I admit things do seem to be piling up against Nick, but Garris said everything is still circumstantial. Don't risk the chief's integrity by convincing him to go against his process."

He slowed down. "Olivia wouldn't admit what she knows about Red and Nick, but did she give you any kind of hint?"

"She only told me that she knows big secrets about them, and she refuses to reveal them."

"Bigger than stealing Trey Connor out from under Red?"

Faith felt the stress of the night dragging her down. "I don't know."

Wolfe resumed his path down the stairway. "Well, I do. I normally don't interfere with guests' conflicts, but if Olivia or anyone else knows why Nick would come after you, then it's high time I stepped in."

Before he could rap on the door of Nick's suite, one of the models rushed toward them. She was tall, blonde, and visibly upset. "Nick's out by the pool, not in his room. But at least you got here fast," she said in a high-pitched, nasal voice that seemed to clash with her posh appearance. "He's really sick. I don't know what happened."

"What?" Faith blurted out.

"About half an hour ago, we were having drinks by the pool, and all of a sudden he collapsed like Olivia did." She turned and headed for the stairs.

Faith caught Wolfe's eye. So Nick was outside, but if what this woman said was true, then it possibly ruled him out from recently tossing bricks through her cottage windows. But did that mean Nick was now a target too?

Faith and Wolfe hurried downstairs.

When they reached the lobby, the night desk clerk came up to them, a local doctor in tow. "We already sent for help, Mr. Jaxon," the clerk said. "I would have told you if I'd known you were awake."

Wolfe glanced from person to person, seemingly as baffled as Faith. "No, that's fine. Please take the doctor out to the pool to see what he can do for Mr. Westfield."

"Poor man," Faith said as they approached the pool and saw how ill Nick appeared. Even though they'd just been suspecting him of doing her harm, his current state gave Faith a pang of sympathy.

The model, however, didn't seem to share Faith's compassion. "It's getting a little creepy around here, isn't it? A slashed dress and tires and a dead guy in the garden. Makes you wonder who's next." She shrugged. "Well, it isn't going to be me. Tell him I hope he's okay, will you? This is all too intense for me." And with that, she went back inside.

"I keep telling myself this event can't get any stranger," Wolfe said. "And I keep being wrong."

"I think this means that Nick couldn't have been the one to break my windows," Faith concluded. "Not in that condition."

"He could be faking his illness," Wolfe suggested.

A pitiful moan came from the pool terrace.

"I highly doubt that," Faith said. "The man is positively green. It had to have been someone else. And short of knocking on every door at this hour, the answer to that will have to wait until morning."

As she took one last glance around, she spotted something. "Look," she said, ushering Wolfe over to the greenery at the far end of the pool. A white cloth was snagged in one of the branches.

The cloth was covered with smears and stains of bright red. At first, Faith thought it was blood, but on closer inspection she realized that it was paint.

It matched the paint on the bricks that had destroyed her windows.

They were all busy, so the cat slipped into the tall woman's room with ease. He'd learned that often the easiest time to search for clues was right under the noses of humans distracted elsewhere.

She had clothes tossed everywhere and lots of photos of herself lying around, but those did not smell like clues. Clues had a most specific smell. There was also a stronger smell in the room, one he didn't recognize. He followed his instincts and went to the fascinating box by the bureau at the far end of the room.

His whiskers told him the source of the strong-smelling clue was in the box, so he hopped up while the woman wasn't watching. In the box were little boxes and bottles and brushes. There were also more of those small paper rectangles, the ones with the red shapes everyone was making a fuss over.

Ah, but there in the back of the box was a small, dark bottle. That one definitely smelled like a clue. The scent was so strong and sour that it wrinkled his nose.

"What are you doing in here?" the woman shrieked. "Get out of my room! Shoo! Go away!" She waved her arms at him.

The cat scampered from the room as fast as he could. But he had seen what he needed to see. He'd have to find a way to bring his human into the room to show her that bottle. Or maybe he'd show it to the nice man from the third floor.

After all, the bottle was an important clue. Any cat worth his tuna could smell that.

9

As much as Faith yearned to question Nick about the suspicious cloth found near him by the pool, it quickly became apparent that the man was too sick to provide any information.

Nick's current state—whether inflicted or self-induced—left Faith and Wolfe little choice but to save the cloth to give to Garris as evidence tomorrow morning.

Watson, who had vanished at some point while they were out by the pool, appeared at Faith's private third-floor guest room door as she settled in for the few hours left until daylight. That was good, because Wolfe demanded she lock it and throw the dead bolt. While Watson had many secret passages, she couldn't be sure he could enter every guest room that way.

Even though Wolfe had wished her at least a few hours' sleep, Faith knew it wouldn't happen. Despite the lavish surroundings, every time she closed her eyes all she could see were the red-stained cloth, the shards of glass, the stark sheets of plywood, and the three bricks.

"What if one of those bricks had hit you, Rumpy? I couldn't stand the idea."

After staring into the dark for half an hour, Faith opened *The Blood of Sisters* to pass the time. If she couldn't sleep, she might as well finish the book. Reading in bed, she dozed perhaps a small amount, but she mostly read the rest of the night.

As the sun came up through the tall windows of the guest room, Faith turned the last page of the book.

"At least something good came out of the time," she said to Watson. "I'll be ready for the book club meeting later. That is, if I can stay awake."

The cat snoozed on the bedspread beside her and didn't respond.

"Are you sure you can't teach me the fine art of catnapping?"

As if to demonstrate, Watson stretched farther out on the bedspread. He glanced at her as if to say, "Learn from the master."

Faith laughed. "You're good company, even if I do envy your dozing. But the sun is up, and some of us have work to do."

Rolling her aching shoulders, she got out of bed, went to the room's balcony doors, and opened them wide. A peach-pink sunrise danced across the waters, visible from this height over the line of trees that separated the manor grounds from the rocky beach and waves.

Craving the exhilaration of the fresh air, Faith walked out onto the balcony in the sweatpants and oversize T-shirt she'd brought as sleepwear.

"You're up," Wolfe said. He stood in the corner of the balcony, which stretched across that side of the third floor.

"I've been up. I'm so up that I'm not sure I slept at all." Faith glanced at him. It wasn't fair how attractive he was even rumpled and unshaven. She ran a hand through the tangle of her hair, pulling it out of the messy ponytail she'd piled on top of her head sometime during the night. Her eyes felt scratchy, and her mouth tasted dry.

He gave her a tender smile. "Am I allowed to say you're adorable under-slept?"

"I'd prefer you tell the truth," she said, padding toward him. The cool moistness of the balcony floor under her bare feet woke her up a bit more, as did the salty tang of the ocean breeze.

"In that case, you are adorably mussed and a surprisingly sweet brand of tired." Wolfe held out his mug of coffee to share.

"Thanks." Faith took a big sip, glad to taste the strength of the brew and feel the mug's warmth radiate against her palms for a moment, then returned the mug to him.

"There's breakfast inside and a pot of strong coffee if you'd like your own mug."

"It sounds wonderful." Faith stretched and let herself enjoy a deep breath of the fresh air. "Everything always feels so peaceful from here." She leaned against the wrought iron balcony.

Wolfe stood next to her, and together they gazed out over the breathtaking scene.

"I used to come here often when I was a boy." He grinned at her. "I'd make up crazy schemes for what I'd do when I owned the manor."

"And now you do," she said.

Wolfe shook his head. "The schemes going on right now are crazier than anything I ever imagined." He reached for her hand. "I want you to take the day off today. Don't go anywhere near Nick or Red or any of the other guests."

"I'll admit I might need a nap," Faith said, yawning. "But what good would it do to hide out?"

"It would keep you safe," he said.

"I've been thinking about that," she replied. "I don't think I'm in any danger."

Wolfe turned to face her. "I couldn't disagree more."

"No, think about it. Last night wasn't meant to harm me. It was a scare tactic. If Nick—or whoever it was—meant to do me actual harm, there were plenty of times when I was alone and far more accessible on the lawn or in the library yesterday."

He gaped at her. "Is that supposed to make me feel better and worry less? At this rate, I've half a mind to close down the library for the rest of the event."

Faith didn't like that idea one bit. "No, don't do that. That would be giving the person behind this exactly what he—or she—wants. A trio of bricks through my window after midnight is theatrical, but that's all it is. I doubt I'm in any real danger."

Wolfe shifted his weight, and she saw the master negotiator in him come to the surface. "I don't agree, but let's follow your line of thinking for a moment. Last night was meant to scare you off. To stop you or anyone else from digging into the recent incidents."

"Yes, that's exactly what I believe."

"So what do you think will happen if you don't back off? Our culprit will have no choice but to escalate things."

"We don't know that," Faith said.

"Don't we?" Wolfe shot back, a new intensity in his eyes. "Olivia went from a shredded dress to physical harm. If it isn't Nick—though I still think it is—then he's been attacked too. And don't forget it all started with a murder. We don't really know who's behind this or why, and that could involve danger for you."

"But—"

Wolfe grasped her shoulders. His eyes were dark. "I can't let anything happen to you. You've got to steer clear of this situation. Stay up here safe and out of the way until Garris works it out. I'll give him the cloth we found last night. You read. Sleep. Stare at the ocean for as long as you like. If you need more company than Watson, I'll send Eileen and Midge to visit with you."

Faith remained silent.

After a long moment, he kissed her forehead and pulled her close. "Please, Faith, let me keep you safe."

It was lovely to rest in his arms, to feel his care and concern. The warmth from his chest chased away all those doubts that had crept in as she watched him talk to the models and socialites. He cared about her deeply. How could she doubt that after the speech he'd just made?

"I'll think about it," Faith finally said, resting her head against his shoulder.

Wolfe pulled away and frowned. "You'll think about it?"

"I've never been one to hide away."

His frown deepened.

"But no one's ever lobbed bricks through my living room

windows before either." With a small smile, Faith added, "In any case, this isn't the kind of decision that should be made on an empty stomach."

He grinned. "I'll feed you eggs and scones until you come around to my point of view, you know."

"Perhaps I'll take the morning off until the final round of the models' competition this afternoon. I really would like to see if Olivia can beat her competition to be the final Connor cover model."

Wolfe opened the door and escorted her to the third-floor dining room, where the smell of breakfast wafted out to entice her.

"That's going to be a fight, I assure you," Wolfe said. "You should have heard those models telling me how each of them was sure they'd nab the final cover. You'd think I was a judge the way they were going on about it."

Faith could only imagine. She'd certainly seen how those women flocked around him. Ironically, one of the things Faith found most attractive about Wolfe was that he had no idea how truly attractive he was. His charisma was completely authentic. It was not at all manufactured like Red's bombastic persona or Nick's salesmanship scheming.

Of course, the models stared at Wolfe as if he were Trey Connor himself. With those looks, that charm, and his financial status, could she blame them?

She must have been too weary to hide her emotions, for Wolfe stopped her in the doorway. "You're not jealous of those models, are you?"

Faith felt herself blush. "They're gorgeous. A man would have to be blind not to be awed. The way they hover around you—"

"Doesn't impress me one bit," he finished for her. "I'm not interested. They're guests, that's all." He cupped her cheek with a gentle hand. "It's you who impresses and amazes me every day."

It wasn't fatigue that made Faith sway a bit. It was the warmth in Wolfe's eyes. She really was falling for this man. And hard.

Faith had to admit that Wolfe had been right, even for the wrong reasons. Spending the morning tucked away on the third floor, soaking in the quiet and the sunshine, had done her a world of good. She'd even slept for an hour or two.

She felt ten times better as she took a seat in the back row of the chairs in the banquet hall for the luncheon that served as the final round of the model competition.

"I heard what happened," Brooke whispered, grabbing Faith's arm as she slipped into a nearby empty chair. "Scary stuff. Are you okay?"

"I'm rattled but all right," Faith replied. "I'd like to think I don't scare so easily."

"Speaking of rattled, Wolfe seems uncharacteristically nervous," Brooke remarked. "I don't blame him. Who would want that job?"

In fact, Wolfe had indeed ended up being a judge in the competition. Nick hadn't recovered enough from whatever had made him sick last night to serve in the role.

In addition, Red was quick to point out that people still suspected the editor of the tire slashing despite his vehement declarations of innocence. Given how much the writer and his editor were at odds, Faith wasn't surprised that Red seemed to take an ungracious pleasure in Nick's misfortune.

If Faith told Red about the cloth, she was almost convinced the author would publicly accuse Nick of the vandalism if not worse. So she and Wolfe left it to Garris to handle.

"Today's final round is a set of interviews," Red said from the podium after announcing the five finalists who had been chosen during yesterday's talent competition.

Olivia sat onstage with the four other models, ready for a series of questions from the panel.

Red smiled. "By the end of the hour, ladies and gentlemen, we'll know who will grace the cover of my final Trey Connor novel."

Faith couldn't help but notice how Red emphasized the word *final*.

"I'm rooting for Olivia, like you," Brooke whispered as the first model made a poor showing of her interview. "She's earned it after all she's been through. I like her style for sticking it out."

The second model handled herself well enough during the interview, but she kept giggling. Faith found it hard to take her seriously. The fact that she kept making eyes at Wolfe didn't earn her points with Faith either, not that she'd admit that to Brooke or anyone else.

The third model was the tall, willowy blonde Faith had met last night in the hallway outside Nick's suite. While she was by far the most attractive of the group, her sharp nasal tone and the jarring high pitch of her voice did her no favors in this segment of the competition.

"I suppose they don't really have to speak on the job much," Faith suggested. "After all, she looks like a princess."

"But she sounds like a seagull," Brooke whispered.

"She's not that bad," Faith replied. Then she quickly filled Brooke in on the red-stained cloth found near Nick last night. "Wolfe told me that when he gave Garris the cloth this morning, the chief said they've still come up dry on the victim's identity."

"Seriously? Nothing?"

Faith shrugged. "They've scoured every missing persons report on the East Coast, and nothing matches our victim's description. They're checking nationally today in the hopes of a match, but Wolfe said Garris didn't sound optimistic."

The model gave another answer in a tone so sharp it was hard to concentrate on her words.

"Can they work with that on a media tour?" Brooke asked, wincing.

Faith glanced at Red, who was clearly taken with the blonde. "Red seems to think they can. And since she was out late by the pool with Nick, I can guess who would have gotten our editor's vote. But what about Wolfe?"

"I hope you told him to vote for Olivia."

"I did no such thing," Faith answered, feigning indignance. Then she grinned. "But I may have mentioned she'd be my choice."

When Olivia finally stepped up for her interview, Faith had to admit she was impressed. Elegant, poised, and beautiful, Olivia was everything Faith thought a Connor cover model should be. A fitting send-off to Red's stellar career. The clear favorite.

Unfortunately, it was equally clear Olivia was not Red's favorite. The tension between the author and the model radiated even to Faith's seat in the back row.

"What is your favorite sports car?" Red asked. The question came out closer to a demand than a query.

The Porsche Olivia named obviously wasn't the answer Red wanted.

"Trey Connor doesn't drive one of those," he snapped at Olivia.

"You didn't ask me what Trey Connor drives," Olivia shot back. "You asked me what my favorite sports car is." She lifted her chin. "Trey Connor drove twelve Jaguars and twelve Lamborghinis."

"I know that," Red growled.

"Is she out to win the cover or put Red in his place?" Brooke whispered.

"The attendees provide the third vote," Faith answered as she scanned the crowd. "I'd say that many of them like Olivia's spunk."

"What do you feel the Trey Connor books have added to American fiction?" Wolfe asked.

Finally, an intelligent question, Faith thought.

"Mr. Maxton has created an American icon," Olivia began. "Trey is suave but not stuffy. He's slick and crafty, but he's always on the side of justice, making him an inspiration to the rest of us to do what is right. Trey Connor is an escape, an adventure, and an ideal all rolled up into one impeccably tailored tuxedo."

"That was a great answer," Brooke said. "Even Red is smiling. Surely she nailed it with that."

"I hope so," Faith said.

They watched as the final model gave her interview.

Then the voting began. Ballot boxes were located at the front of the room for the attendees while Red and Wolfe retreated to another room to confer.

During the break, Eileen appeared in the doorway and waved them over. "Brooke told me what happened to your windows. I can't believe someone would do that to you. I'd be terrified." She gave Faith a big hug. "You and Watson should stay with me until all this blows over."

"Thanks, but I'm okay," Faith replied. "Mack says they'll have temporary windows in place by the end of the day, since it'll be at least a few weeks until the leaded glass ones can be repaired."

She didn't mention her growing suspicions about Nick because she didn't want any attendees to overhear. She planned to fill in the book club later when they met.

The trio approached the refreshments table and helped themselves to elegant glasses of red punch.

"A dead look-alike, slashed tires and a dress, sick people, and now bricks through a window. For a spy contingent, we have way too many unsolved mysteries." Eileen shook her head. "And I usually enjoy solving mysteries."

"We'll figure them out," Faith assured her aunt. "Just as soon as the right clue shows up." She thought about the red-stained cloth. It was paint, not blood, but it could lead to the killer anyway.

"Well, that clue needs to hurry up," Eileen said.

"Where's the real Trey Connor when you need him?" Brooke asked.

"Trey Connor is a spy, not a detective," Faith reminded them. "His job is to take down the bad guy or gain the crucial state secret, not solve a murder or a slashing. Or find out who slipped ipecac into Olivia's and Nick's drinks."

Faith, Brooke, and Eileen stared down at the glasses of red punch in their hands.

"Suddenly I'm not thirsty," Brooke said. "And this is my own recipe."

The women deposited the glasses on a nearby table.

"Take your seats, folks," Red urged from the stage. "We're ready to declare our winner."

"It has to be Olivia," Brooke murmured.

The models returned to their seats onstage.

Olivia's confident expression told Faith the woman felt she was in the lead as well.

After the interviews, Faith didn't see how the audience couldn't come to the same conclusion, and she would guess Wolfe had as well. So even if Red slighted Olivia, she still stood the best chance of being the first and last Connor cover model.

Red smiled. "It's with great pleasure that I introduce you to Trey Connor's final cover beauty." He paused dramatically before announcing, "Denise Conley!"

The beautiful model with the jarring voice rose and waved to the crowd. She glided over to Red and stood beside him.

Brooke turned to Faith. "Well, you said there probably isn't much talking involved, but still."

"Maybe the crowd picked up on how much Red liked her," Faith replied, surprised and disappointed by the decision.

"Are you sure you want to do that?" Olivia called out.

"Of course I am," Red challenged.

"How about after I tell you I found a bottle of syrup of ipecac in Denise's makeup case?" Olivia held up a small bottle. "It's what made me sick at the reception."

A few members of the crowd gasped.

Olivia whirled around to Denise. "You were with Nick Westfield last night, and now he's sick. This bottle is half-empty. What do you say to that?"

10

"**I** didn't make Nick sick!" Denise shouted. "I didn't!"

Olivia rushed over to Denise and thrust the bottle in her face. "This was in your makeup case. It's obviously yours."

Denise glanced around the room, her long form practically folding in on itself. "Maybe."

The audience started murmuring.

"But I swear I didn't use it on you or Nick," Denise added.

Red backed away from Denise in a not-so-subtle move. "You just happened to have a bottle of that stuff in your makeup case?"

"Find me a model who doesn't," Denise challenged. She gazed pleadingly at the other models.

"I think we should take this into another room," Wolfe interjected. "Guests, please enjoy the refreshments, and don't forget to join us for the next event later today." Then he swiftly ushered Olivia, Denise, and Red out of the room.

"We're certainly glad you're all right," Midge told Faith. "Any of those bricks could have hit you or Watson."

Faith, Brooke, Midge, and Eileen were gathered around a table of luscious desserts at Snickerdoodles Bakery & Tea Shop later that afternoon. The bakery's enticing selection of sweets and its convenient location right next to the library made it a favorite meeting spot for book club social gatherings.

"It's unnerving," Faith admitted as she warmed her hands on her coffee mug. Everyone at the manor had begun to think twice about their beverages since Olivia and Nick had taken ill. The bakery's good coffee aside, it was nice to go somewhere she could sip in complete confidence. "But I've given it a lot of thought, and I'm sure those bricks were meant to scare me, not harm me."

"Who would want to scare you and why?" Midge asked, sinking her fork into a slice of chocolate cake. "You don't have anything to do with Red's retirement party."

Faith set down her coffee and began ticking facts off on her fingers. "I saw Nick Westfield, Red's editor, near the show cars before we discovered their tires were slashed. I found all those playing cards in his glove box. I saw the body in the hedge maze. And while I tried to hide it, Nick probably knows I overheard an argument he had with Red in the library. He must realize that I suspect him."

"Nick threw the bricks to keep you quiet?" Eileen asked. She removed her knitting project from her tote and set to work.

Faith nodded. "He seems to have the most reason. I did overhear him admit to trying to continue the Trey Connor series without Red."

"But Nick got sick too," Brooke pointed out. "So it can't be him."

"That's the one thing I can't figure out," Faith said. "It's possible he made himself sick to create a good alibi."

Brooke broke off a piece of her lemon pound cake. "Does that mean Nick is behind all the other incidents? The three of diamonds card was left on everything."

"While the evidence points to Nick, it's still circumstantial," Midge said. "Those cards would be awfully easy to get or to copy. And more than one person could have thought of it, given how they figure so prominently in Red's books."

"There wasn't a card left with Olivia's and Nick's drinks," Faith said, thinking aloud. "Although it's clear to see how that model Denise tainted those, isn't it?"

"Surely Denise confessed once Olivia found the drug in her makeup case, right?" Midge asked.

"Actually, no," Faith answered. "Just like Nick, Denise swore she was innocent. She admitted it was her bottle—she says models use the stuff all the time to reduce their appetites of all the awful things—but even when Garris pressed her, she denied using it on Nick or Olivia."

Brooke made a face. "Horrible but plausible."

Midge frowned. "You don't believe her denial, do you?"

"No, I don't, so I'm glad Garris took the bottle in as evidence along with the cloth Wolfe and I found," Faith said. "After all, Denise had reason to hurt Olivia's chances of winning the competition, and she was at the reception when Olivia became ill. She's also the only person who was with Nick when he got sick."

"Syrup of ipecac acts very quickly, doesn't it?" Brooke asked.

"Within about ten minutes," Midge said. "And it tastes horrid. I don't know how either of them didn't notice it in their drinks. It's really nasty stuff."

Eileen paused in her knitting. "We can't forget that Nick was also in both those places."

"What if Nick and Denise are working together?" Midge suggested. "It would explain why she won the competition. Maybe Nick fixed it."

Brooke shook her head. "I can't imagine anyone doing that to themselves. If Nick did throw those bricks through the cottage windows, there are plenty of better alibis than making himself ill."

"Nick has a stock of three of diamonds cards," Eileen added.

"But that's not much evidence," Midge said. "It makes sense that he'd have them. They are Trey's signature after all, and I'm sure they regularly use the cards for promotions and such."

"I doubt they'll be using them much anymore," Brooke remarked. "Having your trademark found with a dead body sort of ruins the appeal."

"And what about that body?" Eileen asked. "Nick's clearly our main suspect, but we haven't connected him to the murder yet. Have they even learned who the victim was?"

"Not that I know of," Faith said.

"I can't get over the fact that the man in the hedge resembled Red so much," Brooke said.

"It's very strange," Eileen agreed. "Remember in *The Blood of Sisters* when the chemist found a clue in the forensic report?"

Midge nodded. "I wish we could see the report for our John Doe. Maybe it would help us identify him."

"Do you think Garris would show it to us?" Brooke asked.

"I doubt it," Faith said.

"It's worth a shot," Brooke said. "I think I'll ask Garris about it anyway."

Jane McGee, the bakery owner, walked over to their table. "Were you talking about those three of diamonds playing cards?"

"We were," Faith answered. "Why?"

Jane held up a three of diamonds card. "They started showing up around town today." She turned to Eileen. "Did you get one at the library?"

Eileen shook her head. "Where else have they been found?"

"A burned card was left beside the cash register at the candle shop," Jane said. "At the yarn shop, a card was stabbed with a pair of knitting needles. I'll bet there are others too."

"Where was yours?" Brooke asked.

"A customer found it tucked under a scone in the display case about an hour ago," Jane replied.

"Everyone from the event, including Nick, is supposed to be at a lecture right now," Faith said. "Who has time to be running around dropping mysterious cards all over Lighthouse Bay?"

"And why?" Midge asked as she grabbed her phone. "I'm calling Sarah to see if a card has appeared over there. This is getting creepy."

Sarah Goodwin was the store manager at Happy Tails and Midge's most trusted employee.

"May I see your card?" Faith asked.

Jane handed it to her.

Sure enough, Jane's card had the same design on the back as the dozens that had spilled out of Nick's glove box. If this new mystery card "dealer" was Nick, he'd recovered fast enough to make Faith believe he actually could have faked his condition last night. But why spread the mystery into town?

"Yep," Midge said, ending the call. "One showed up in the bakery fifteen minutes ago. It was stuck in one of the dog toys. I'd better get over there." The veterinarian began gathering her things.

"Our murderer is leaving dramatic and literal calling cards." Eileen cringed. "This is starting to sound like one of the maniacal evil geniuses in a Trey Connor novel."

Midge waved as she hurried out the door.

A moment later, Seth Cole from the library rushed inside. "We need you back at the library," he said to Eileen. "A patron found some guy attacking the stacks, and we've called the police."

Eileen hurriedly put away her knitting. "Attacking the stacks? How?"

"He was ripping pages out of a bunch of paperbacks in the back of the library," Seth explained. "He piled them up and put a playing card on top. One of the patrons saw him doing it and ran to the front desk."

"Let me guess," Eileen said as she stood. "A three of diamonds atop a stack of Trey Connor novels?"

Seth's eyes grew wide. "How did you know?"

"He's been doing it around town," Jane said.

"And now we've got him," Eileen said victoriously.

Faith and Brooke followed her to the library to see the culprit caught red-handed.

"Dead body?" A skinny young man gawked at Chief Garris. "I only did the cards. I don't know anything about a murder."

After a pause, the chief said, "Mr. Everett, I didn't mention a murder." The man swallowed hard.

Faith felt her stomach drop. Was this man, who offered no rationale for his strange behavior, the murderer?

Chief Garris had ushered Faith, Eileen, and Brooke into one of the library meeting rooms, where he was questioning Stuart Everett about the playing cards. Stuart sat at the long table, fidgeting nervously, and Officer Tobin stood at the door.

"Well, people have been talking up at the manor that some kind of Red impersonator was murdered," Stuart mumbled.

As explanations went, Faith thought this one didn't hold much water.

"Are you a guest at the manor?" Garris asked suspiciously.

Faith could have answered for him. She hadn't seen this man before, and she would have remembered his unique features. He was young, very tall, and dressed in dark colors. His thick-rimmed tortoiseshell glasses magnified his dark eyes. He had the unmistakable appearance of a young and struggling city dweller, whereas the guests had an almost uniform country-club posh. And Stuart certainly lacked the casual coastal style of most people around Lighthouse Bay.

"Do I look like one of those rich-and-mighty types?" Stuart said, echoing Faith's thoughts. He raised his chin defiantly. "They don't let just anyone into that private circle, you know."

The chief walked slowly around the table. "Got a beef with Trey Connor fans, do you?"

"I *am* a Trey Connor fan," Stuart proclaimed. "A huge fan like the ones at the manor. But the only people who get to say goodbye to—or even get near—Red Maxton are the ones with deep enough pockets. The rest of us like Trey Connor as much as they do, but we don't seem to matter at all."

"If you like his books, ripping them up is a poor way of showing it," Eileen said. "You destroyed our property, and you've been scaring people around town. What on earth did you hope to accomplish by doing that?"

Stuart offered no answer.

Faith was unable to conjure up an explanation for his actions. Stuart was articulate, and he seemed too intelligent to lash out or cause a disruption for no reason. Then again, people often behaved in ways that didn't make sense.

"So you're not a guest," Garris said. "But have you been at or near Castleton Manor anytime in the last week?"

Stuart ran his hands down his face, his earlier composure apparently starting to unravel. "Maybe."

The chief leaned over Stuart. "Maybe how?"

"I knew Nick would never let me in, so I had to settle for watching from a distance," Stuart answered. "The edge of the grounds and such."

"The grounds where the show cars were parked?" Faith asked. "On Sunday, perhaps? In possession of a knife big enough to slash tires?"

"I didn't do that," Stuart insisted.

"Didn't you?" Garris pressed.

"No!" Stuart shouted. "Believe me, I don't like those people and their airs, but I wouldn't damage their cars."

"But apparently our books are fair game," Eileen said sharply.

"Were you inside Castleton Manor anytime this week?" the chief asked.

"Once," Stuart admitted. "I went to the gift shop to buy a coffee."

Faith knew that Marlene would be irritated to learn someone who wasn't a guest got as far as the coffee and gift shop when the manor wasn't hosting a public event.

"What day was that?" Garris asked.

"Saturday."

"The day Olivia Bishop's dress was slashed," Faith said.

She couldn't see how Stuart had managed to waltz into the manor off the street, make his way to the second floor, get inside Olivia's suite, and destroy her dress without anyone noticing. Still, Faith had to admit that it was certainly possible.

"The first cover model?" Stuart asked. "Who did they choose for the final cover? They did that today, didn't they?"

The chief frowned. "I'm not here to update you on Trey Connor trivia. This isn't a fan club meeting."

"Did you throw bricks through my cottage window last night?" Faith demanded. Considering what Stuart had been doing around town today, it didn't seem like a stretch that he was the one who had lobbed those bricks into her home. Perhaps it hadn't been Nick after all.

Stuart stared at her from behind his thick glasses. "Why would I do that? I don't even know who you are."

Faith didn't care for the disdain in his voice. "It seems as though you don't know who anyone in Lighthouse Bay is, yet you seem perfectly content to scare us all. Why?"

Garris motioned for Stuart to get up. "You're going to come down to the station and give a full statement on the playing cards and where you left them."

"Not to mention pay for the damages done at the library," Eileen said. "And elsewhere."

Officer Tobin walked over and took Stuart by the arm.

"Wait a minute." Stuart gulped. "I know my rights. Don't I get a phone call first?"

"It had better be to someone who can verify your whereabouts last Thursday night," the chief said. "Right now, you're not only charged with vandalism, but you're a pretty likely suspect for murder."

"But I didn't kill anyone," Stuart replied. "I'm here for work."

Garris cocked his head. "What do you mean?"

"I work for Nick Westfield."

Stuart was an employee of Red's publishing house? Faith found that a highly interesting development.

The chief ignored Stuart's comment and turned to Eileen. "Give me a full accounting of the damages done. We'll contact the other businesses in town to do the same." He glanced at Stuart. "Hopefully a serious conversation with our Mr. Everett here will solve what's been going on around town and at the manor."

Garris and Tobin led Stuart out the door.

Faith, Eileen, and Brooke stared after the trio.

"I can see him slashing the tires or somehow getting close enough to go after Nick and Olivia," Eileen said. "But why bother with us? Why the library and Snickerdoodles and the other businesses? It doesn't make sense."

Faith gathered her handbag. "There's only one person who can make sense of all this. Nick Westfield."

Eileen's eyes widened. "You're not going to confront him with the murder, are you? He could be dangerous."

"No, I'll leave that to Garris. But I can ask him about the cloth we found and what kind of work Stuart does for him." She headed for the door. "It's time to have a chat with Nick. Whether he's ready or not."

11

Nick appeared a little green around the gills when he opened the door to his suite.

Faith decided to start with the less confrontational issue. "I've just met Stuart Everett, and it's not under good circumstances. We need to talk."

"He's here?" Nick sighed heavily.

Faith stared at him. She'd expected the editor to deny knowing Stuart. Were Stuart's claims legitimate?

Nick motioned her into the room. "What did Stuart do?"

"The police picked him up in Lighthouse Bay for leaving threatening three of diamonds cards all over town," Faith said as she walked inside. "And tearing pages out of every Trey Connor novel in our town's library."

Nick groaned. He didn't reply and instead walked through the French doors and out onto the balcony.

Faith followed him onto the balcony. As she scanned the view, she saw the three finalist cars parked for today's final judging on the lawn.

Most of the car owners had scrambled to repair or replace their vehicle's damaged tires. In light of what had happened, the group agreed not to include tire condition in the stringent criteria for choosing the winning car. But they also agreed to remove Nick as a judge, once again calling on Wolfe to step in.

Faith could see Wolfe on the lawn now, peering into one of the vehicle's interiors as he inspected the car.

"Stuart told Chief Garris that he's here working for you," Faith said. Nick remained silent.

"I'm assuming that the explanation is complicated," Faith continued. "So Stuart didn't explain why he was here?" Nick asked.

"No. He only said it was for work."

Nick finally turned to face Faith. "I'm not sure I can explain his presence. Stuart does work for me, but I assure you that he's not here working for me."

"What exactly does Stuart do for you?" she asked.

Nick tucked his hands into his pockets. "I'm surprised Stuart didn't blurt it out under those circumstances. He's never liked my requirement for secrecy, despite how well I pay him."

Complicated answer indeed, Faith thought. "Meaning?"

"When a writer comes to me with solid promise or a great story but their technique isn't up to snuff, we call in a book doctor. The book doctor works closely with a writer to bring the book to publication standards. Sometimes it's practically rewriting the whole thing for the person, especially if it's a celebrity."

Faith had met enough celebrity authors to be familiar with the reality that many of them barely wrote their own books. "And Stuart is one of your book doctors?"

"He is."

"For Red?"

Nick laughed. "No. Even if Red needed a book doctor, I doubt he'd ever submit to one. I think you can probably guess I've had more than my share of editorial arguments with the man."

She nodded. Given Red's volatile personality and their argument she'd overheard, it wasn't hard to believe. "Then what does Stuart have to do with the Trey Connor books?"

Nick walked back into the room. "Well, that's the secret part."

Faith followed him. "Someone's been killed, you and Olivia have been sickened, my home has been vandalized, tires and a dress have been slashed, and my town has been harassed by one of your employees. If this is about your plans to pull another author into the Trey Connor franchise, I think it's time you come clean about it."

Nick didn't respond.

"You should know that we found a cloth with red paint in the bushes by the pool where Denise led us to your medical episode."

He still didn't reply.

Faith took a deep breath and plunged ahead. "Does Stuart's work for you include throwing bricks painted with red diamonds through my living room windows? Or did you do it?"

"What?" Nick said, his face coming alive at the accusation. "No! I had nothing to do with that."

Faith didn't know if she believed him. "Chief Garris will probably get it out of Stuart even if you don't admit it to me."

Nick collapsed into a chair and sighed. "You're right."

Faith sat down in a chair opposite Nick and studied him. His confession seemed much too easy.

"You're right about Stuart but not the bricks," he clarified. "I would think the condition you saw me in last night should be proof enough that I couldn't have done that."

Faith offered no reply. Just because Nick appeared ill didn't mean someone else had made him so. And he could have paid someone to throw the bricks through her windows.

"I do have plans to bring in another author to replace Red," Nick admitted. "But it had to be exactly the right author. Shortly after Red announced his plans to retire, Stuart told me he had the perfect writer to step into Red's shoes to continue the Trey Connor series."

"You've already told me Red would never agree to something like that."

"Difficult isn't the same as impossible," Nick pointed out. "I dismissed Stuart's idea at first, thinking he'd invented this perfect spy writer in an attempt to further his own career."

"You wouldn't want Stuart to be the writer to step in?" Faith asked.

"I hope this event has shown you that it's about more than writing. Red's ability to take on that suave persona everyone knows and loves is as much of an asset as his writing talent. You've met Stuart. I told him he doesn't quite give off the vibe Trey's author needs to have."

Faith blinked. "Are you saying you told Stuart he isn't debonair enough to write Trey Connor novels?"

Nick gestured toward the lawn. "This isn't a fair business. Talent is certainly key, but even that is not always necessary with people like Stuart in the picture. These days a great book is really only half the recipe for success."

"You need an author who can do what it takes to sell books," Faith finished for him.

Nick nodded. "Trey's author needs to be a man of style and sophistication. Look at Red. He's terrified someone's out to kill him, but he still manages to play the larger-than-life dynamo. Can you see Stuart pulling that off?"

No, Faith thought. *At least not nearly as well as Red does it.*

"Now you've got me wondering if Stuart's stunts weren't misguided attempts to try and be larger than life." Nick shook his head. "He's got it all wrong. Always did."

"But Stuart told you he'd found someone who was an ideal replacement for Red," she reminded him.

"He told me the person has the personality, but we disagreed on the writing chops. Stuart brought me a rough draft of his mysterious writer's manuscript. He said that if I'd agree to pay him to doctor the book to publication standards, he'd produce this author he swore was worthy to step into Red's shoes."

"And you agreed?" Faith found it disrespectful to Red at best, deceptive at worst. This only added to the pile of reasons to suspect Nick as the man behind everything that had been happening.

"I told him I'd consider it. I didn't take Stuart entirely seriously, though. If nothing else, I thought that it would give me enough time to bring Red around to the idea."

Faith folded her arms across her chest. "I can't see Red ever agreeing to it."

"I'm aware that you overheard our conversation, so you know there's a movie deal in the works if we can produce three more books." Nick leaned forward. "I'll need you to keep quiet about that."

There was enough edge to the editor's voice to make Faith believe the man in front of her could have slashed tires or the gown or tossed bricks through her window. She nodded.

"The Trey Connor franchise is worth a lot of money," Nick went on. "Sure, Stuart's scheme was far-fetched, but if we could have gotten it to work, I believed it could have solved everyone's problems. So to me, it was a risk worth taking."

She noticed Nick used the past tense. "What happened?"

"I got nervous when I hadn't heard from Stuart, and I asked him for some sample revised chapters. They'd have to be brilliant, you understand. So brilliant that Red would be more impressed than threatened."

"And were they?" Faith asked.

"No, but Stuart had a different opinion. I told him he'd have to step up his game. Maybe that's what he thought he was doing with those playing cards."

"Did you tell him anything else?"

"I said that he'd have to produce an author that could fill Red's shoes beyond our expectations," Nick answered. "Even more Red than Red was, if you will. It had to be both a great book and a charismatic author to go forward."

"Do you think Stuart was putting playing cards all over Lighthouse Bay in an attempt to be charismatic?" Faith asked.

"I admit, it doesn't make much sense to me. Stuart is disgruntled and artistic, but I'd like to think even he has enough sense to know that stunts like that won't help him." Nick paused, as if deciding whether to say his next words. "I have to wonder. What if the guy in your hedge maze was Stuart's mystery writer? After all, what's more Red than someone who looks exactly like Red?"

Faith shivered. Would the man who committed the murder ask such a question to deflect suspicion? She couldn't say. "That seems unlikely."

"Not if you think about it," Nick said. "Stuart knows we're on a deadline to produce that book. What if he thought he could back me into a corner by delivering the book but not the author?"

The theory made enough sense that Faith's spine iced over. "If Stuart thought removing his stand-in for Red could fix it so he was your only option . . ." She didn't finish the sentence. It was extreme, but so was the scheme Stuart had already hatched.

"I guess it's hard to believe someone you work with could be conniving enough to pull off something like this," Nick said.

"Stuart knew about the murder before Garris mentioned it," Faith said. "And he was clever enough to be right here under your nose without you knowing it."

Before Nick could respond, a loud cheer went up from the grounds. Nick stood up and walked out the French doors.

Faith followed him to the balcony and saw the guests crowded around Red. Whatever he was doing, he held them all enthralled.

"You'd never know Red is terrified someone's out to get him, would you?" Nick asked.

"He definitely hides it well," Faith answered. "You're right about Stuart. I'm not sure he could handle it."

"But he's obviously trying." Nick sighed. "It's ironic that Stuart's finally impressed me. Only it's in all the wrong ways."

As Faith left the room, she wondered if Nick had just come up with a likely motive for Stuart as the murderer.

Or deftly deflected suspicion from himself.

The manor's stately Great Hall Gallery was lavishly decorated to resemble a Trey Connor art exhibit. Faith, Wolfe, and Marlene walked down the long hallway right before the evening's reception when the winner of the car show would be announced. Faith had left Watson snoozing in the library.

"It was harder than you'd think to pick the winner," Wolfe remarked. "There were so many incredible cars out there."

Denise had done a photo shoot with the three finalist cars. As a result, a display of photographs now graced the walls of the gallery, showcasing Denise with each of the vehicles. It was a preview of potential Trey Connor covers.

"I don't understand," Marlene said as she studied the images. "The books are about Trey Connor. Why isn't he in these photographs?"

"I asked Red about that," Wolfe replied. "He said they don't show Trey on the cover because every man wants to imagine he's Trey."

"That's ridiculous," Marlene scoffed.

"That's marketing," Wolfe said. "And while it may sound ridiculous to you, Red's laughing all the way to a well-financed retirement."

After hearing Red's arguments with Nick and learning about the strife Stuart had faced while trying to launch his own writing career, Faith could see how Red could grow weary of the business. It was clear that he no longer enjoyed writing the books. Most people probably thought Red got to call all the shots in his career, but Faith was discovering that wasn't quite true. Much of it was an act.

Marlene glanced at the other end of the gallery. "They're about to get started. I'd better make sure everything is in order," she declared, then strode away.

"Which car is your favorite?" Wolfe asked Faith as they stood back to view the glamorous photos.

In truth, they all looked pretty much the same to Faith. "The dark blue car," she said. "It reminds me of yours."

Wolfe smiled. "What do you know? That's my favorite too."

He raised his arms to show off a set of cuff links that were small enamel playing cards with red jewels for the three of diamonds. "A gift from Red for helping with the competitions."

For a moment, Faith thought that were he in possession of writing talent, Wolfe might be the ideal man to step into Red's shoes as the author of the Trey Connor books.

"Lucky me. I win no matter which car takes first place," Denise said as she glided over to them.

"I'm sure it will be a big boost to your career," Wolfe said. "Trey's final adventure will undoubtedly fly off the shelves."

"I was telling Red I should do the next movies." Denise struck a dramatic pose. "I'm in acting school."

"Impressive," Wolfe replied politely. He glanced toward the other end of the gallery. "I think they're starting."

Denise's gaze followed his. "Yes, we are. Excuse me. I get to hand over the trophy."

Faith stared after Denise as the model made her way to the stage at the front of the room and stood between Red and Nick. "I can't believe they still let her do the shoots with everything that's happened. That horrid syrup."

"Just because she owned a bottle doesn't mean she gave it to Olivia or Nick," Wolfe reasoned. "It makes her foolish to use it, but it doesn't make her guilty unless they can prove her bottle was used in those drinks. And Garris says he can't."

"Ladies and gentlemen," Nick called, "gather at this end of the room if you would. We'll kick off the party with the announcement you've all been waiting for."

Faith and Wolfe joined the assembled group.

"The guaranteed spot on the cover of the next Trey Connor novel goes to . . ." Nick paused dramatically.

Faith noticed Nick said "next" instead of "final," which only reminded her how determined the editor was to have his way.

Judging by the glower on Red's face, he hadn't missed it either.

"The gorgeous 1950 Jaguar XK120 alloy roadster." Nick pointed to the photo of the car that had been carefully unloaded out of the trailer.

The crowd applauded, and Denise smiled and raised the trophy.

"It's one of the most beautiful cars I've ever seen," Wolfe said. "And it's in fabulous condition. I can't wait to meet the owner."

"Didn't you meet him while you were viewing the car?" Faith asked.

"No. It was delivered by a broker," Wolfe replied. "But he told me the owner would be here for the party tonight."

"Would the owner of this extraordinary vehicle come up and claim the honor?" Nick called out, scanning the crowd.

"I most certainly will," came a woman's voice from the back of the room. "Clear a path, darlings."

Everyone turned to see a woman in a white cocktail dress pushing through the crowd. The woman had short red hair, and she wore sunglasses, a broad hat, bloodred lipstick, and wickedly high heels. If any Trey Connor novel had featured a female supervillain, Faith imagined the character would be very much like this mysterious guest.

The woman smiled at Denise. "I'm so glad that you'll be posing with my car." She glared at Olivia. "Because I'd do anything to keep you off the cover of the last Trey Connor book."

Red let out a string of curses that sent the room into shock.

Nick seemed stunned. He made an attempt to hold Red back, but he was too late.

Red stormed toward the red-haired woman with a startling fire in his eyes. "Angela, get out of my party."

"But I just won." Spite dripped from her words as she removed her sunglasses to glare at Red.

"Over my dead body!" Red yelled. "Nothing you own—bought with my money, no doubt—will ever show up on my cover."

Angela was petite compared to Red, but she marched right up

to him and lifted her chin defiantly. "I do believe I heard the word *guaranteed* come out of your editor's mouth." She waved hands with long red-lacquered fingernails around the room. "All these witnesses, you know."

"Never," Red growled. "Crawl back under your rock. Your tricks won't work here."

"Now is that any way to treat a lady?" Angela tried to sidestep Red to reach the stage.

But the author blocked her way. "You're no lady."

"Ladies and gentlemen," Nick cut in loudly, rushing to where the two stood squaring off. "Enjoy the refreshments while I take Red and his ex-wife into another room to settle down." The editor pulled Red in the direction of the library.

Faith dashed out ahead of them to open the door and perhaps secure anything that could be used as a weapon.

12

"What in the world are you doing here?" Red roared at Angela.

Faith and Wolfe stood in the library with Red, Nick, and Angela.

Watson, clever cat that he was, took the commotion as his cue to swiftly exit the library.

Faith wished she could follow her cat, given the battle that was brewing.

"Exactly what it looks like," Angela purred. "I'm getting on the last cover. Or at least my car is."

"Your car?" Red said. "That can't be your car. You don't even care about cars."

"Well, no," Angela said as she ran her finger across the back of one of the chairs in front of the fireplace. "But I'm very fond of revenge. And this was delicious. It was worth every dollar."

"Every one of *my* dollars, you mean," Red scoffed.

"She must really hate him," Wolfe whispered as he and Faith kept a safe distance away from the angry pair.

"It seems mutual," Faith replied.

Nick stepped between them, even though his expression said he'd rather face another round of tainted drinks than try to keep these two from fighting. "Angela, you can't think we'll agree to—"

"To keep your word?" Angela interrupted. "To make good on your little publicity stunt out there?"

"Go home," Red snarled.

Angela ignored Red and turned to Nick. "She's very pretty, by the way. You're clearly moving up in the world."

Faith shivered. Angela not only resembled an evil villain, but she seemed to have the personality to match.

"That's enough," Red told her. "Get out of here. You've had your fun."

Angela grinned. "Oh, I'm only getting started. I'm going to make sure you go out with a whimper, not a bang."

"You're not an invited guest," Nick reminded her. "That means you're trespassing. If you leave right now, I won't ask Mr. Jaxon to call the police."

"This is your place?" Angela walked toward Wolfe. "Well done. Terribly classy. Exactly the sort of thing Red loves. Tell me about all that's gone wrong with his little goodbye party. One hears rumors. A dead body in the garden is so dramatic."

"Where did you hear that?" Red demanded.

"Wouldn't you like to know?" Angela sneered. "You're not the only one capable of a good plot twist. Or a cliff-hanger. Let's just say I stay informed. After all, not all our friends hate me as much as you do."

"So help me, if you don't get out of here right now—"

Wolfe stepped forward. "Mrs. Maxton, why don't I show you to your car?"

"It's Gander now, dear," Angela said. "I dropped the Maxton name."

"But you kept your clutches on the Maxton money," Red snapped.

"Ms. Gander," Wolfe corrected, "I'll arrange for an off-site meeting between you and Mr. Westfield for tomorrow to talk about the cover and your extraordinary car. But for tonight, I really must insist you leave as quietly as possible for the sake of our guests."

Angela nodded, then shot Red one of the nastiest looks Faith had ever seen. "Watch your back. You never know what someone might do to you on your way out of the limelight."

Wolfe steered Angela out the door.

When they were gone, Red jabbed a finger at Nick. "If you put that car on my book, I'll burn down your publishing house." He stormed from the room.

Nick slumped against a bookshelf and sighed. "Believe it or not, I used to love my job."

It was late by the time the reception ended. The day's full dose of drama had been more than enough, but on top of everything else that had happened, Faith was overwhelmed. All she wanted to do was collect Watson and go home. The quiet of her cottage seemed a far better choice than the tense air in the manor tonight.

"I don't like it," Wolfe said when she told him where she planned to sleep. "I'd feel much better if you stayed in the manor again."

Faith was sure if it were anyone other than her, he might insist. Thankfully, he knew her well enough not to do that. Or so she hoped. She reminded herself that it had been a long day and an even longer night. They both had frayed nerves.

"I'll be fine," she assured him. "The temporary windows are installed, and the leaded glass ones will go back in as soon as they're ready."

"It's not about windows," Wolfe said. "It's about you. I want you safe. And for me, safe means staying here under this roof."

Faith loved his concern, but she'd barely slept last night and doubted the strained atmosphere around the manor would help one bit. "I know you do, but I'm tired and I want my own bed."

Watson appeared at her side as if to say, "Me too."

Wolfe paced the library. "We can't prove Nick threw those bricks or slashed the tires. We still don't know who killed the man in the hedge or how Angela got onto the grounds without anyone noticing. I don't feel right about your being out there in the cottage all alone."

Watson walked up to Wolfe, seeming to take offense that his company didn't count.

Faith was tired enough for Wolfe's comment to strike a nerve. "I'm entirely capable of taking care of myself. Watson and I have lived on our own for years. And in case you've forgotten, I've faced some pretty tricky circumstances in my time here and come out fine."

Wolfe obviously caught the edge in her tone. He stopped pacing and put his hand to his forehead, wincing. "Why won't you let me help you?" His question came dangerously close to a demand.

Faith closed her eyes and silently counted to five. "I don't want to argue about this."

"Then don't," he replied. "Stay here."

She folded her arms across her chest. "I stayed until the temporary windows were in. Now I'm more tired than scared, and I want to go back to the cottage."

He glared at her, clearly biting back a retort. His nerves were strung as tight as hers. This was going to escalate into an argument they'd both regret.

"The cottage is my home," Faith said with as much calm as she could muster. "I'm not going to let Nick or anyone else scare me out of it. Besides, I think I'd feel safer not being under the same roof as Nick Westfield right now."

Wolfe threw his hands up in the air. "How am I supposed to protect you?"

Faith bit her lip in frustration. She needed her own space and her familiar bed with Watson curled at her feet. "We're both tired. This has been a trying night. Don't let this be the first thing we fight about."

He started to say something, then stopped. He made several more such attempts before he managed to say, "I will walk you home."

Now that was a demand she could live with. "Thank you," she said as she picked up her purse.

"And you will throw the dead bolt on your door," he added.

She could almost smile, even if he couldn't quite yet. "Of course."

"You will also be sure to call me at the first sign of any danger, even if you think it's nothing," Wolfe went on. "Especially if you think it's nothing."

"Absolutely," Faith said as they left the library with Watson trotting beside them.

"Will you meet me for breakfast before we have to set up the gadget exhibition in the library tomorrow morning?" he asked.

The gadget exhibition. The last program of an event Faith was very impatient to end. "I'll consider it. But I believe we'd both be better served by sleeping in, don't you think?"

Wolfe studied her as they walked. "My mother always used to say a woman with a strong spine was worth two with a pretty face." There was a hint of the familiar sparkle in his eyes.

Hoping this argument had run its course, Faith asked, "Do you think she's right?"

Wolfe grinned. "I'll let you know."

It would have felt satisfying to say she'd gotten a wonderful night's sleep in her own bed, but Faith slept only a few hours before Wednesday morning dawned. The old cottage had always been a creaky home, and she couldn't help but hear every single noise. It felt like peaceful sleep dangled just out of her reach. By the day's first light, Faith wasn't sure her insistence on standing her ground in the cottage had been the wisest choice.

She'd begged off having breakfast with Wolfe, preferring to nurse her tired doubts in the quiet of her own kitchen and with a long, hot shower. Then she grabbed her copy of *The Blood of Sisters*. She planned to pass the book along to another member of the staff who'd asked to read it.

"I have no idea what today will bring," Faith said to Watson as they left the cottage. "I know that's true every day, but with all that's happened this week, it feels even truer today."

Still, she was thankful for the familiarity of their usual commute across the grounds to the manor. Even though she'd gotten precious little sleep, she could declare to Wolfe that she'd passed the night without incident or harm.

As she and Watson passed the hedge maze that started all the chaos, Faith said a brief prayer for the as-yet-unidentified body that had been found there. Someone somewhere was that man's mother or father or sister or brother. Were his family members searching for him? Distraught by his disappearance? It seemed a sad thing that a man's life could be snuffed out with none of his loved ones even aware that he was gone.

Was he Stuart's mystery author? And if so, how was it that Stuart didn't know his crucial writing partner was here and that he was dead?

A playful bark echoed from the direction of the manor, pulling Faith from her thoughts. She turned to see Red struggling to hold Rufus back. The exuberant dog had caught sight of Watson, and he was straining at his leash to reach the cat.

Watson didn't wait around to see if Rufus considered him a playmate or puppy food. With one glance in the direction of the dog, the cat was off like a black-and-white streak into the maze and out of sight.

"Sorry to scare off your cat like that," Red said as he approached, still grappling to restrain Rufus's enthusiasm for the chase.

The dog clearly wanted to play hide-and-seek in the hedge maze, and Faith was glad Red showed no signs of letting him.

"Oh, Watson's fine," Faith said, reaching down to distract the dog with a vigorous scratch behind the ears.

Rufus rewarded her greeting with a smile and a big, sloppy lick that made her laugh. Cats were clever and quiet, but there was something to be said for the loyal exuberance of a dog.

"Watson knows a hundred ways into and out of the manor," Faith continued. "I have no doubt he'll be sitting on my desk waiting for me when I get there."

"Intelligent animal." Red began walking alongside Faith with Rufus in tow. "I'm a dog man myself, but I can appreciate a good feline companion. Your Watson seems like a nice fellow."

Faith nodded. "He was a rescue, but it's one of those stories where it's difficult to say who rescued who."

It was true. She had been struggling with the loss of her grandmother when she found Watson as a kitten. Rescuing the shivering little kitten out of the snowy night had given Faith somewhere to send all the love she could no longer give to her grandmother. The cat had been her unwavering companion and comfort for many wonderful years. Watson was, quite simply, family.

"I know the feeling," Red replied. "I got Rufus as a puppy when things fell apart with my ex-wife you met last night. He kept me going at a tough time. I feel the same way about Rufus as I expect you do about Watson."

"I'm sorry things got so out of hand with the car show award," Faith said, recalling the dramatic scene when Angela had arrived and how mean-spirited she had been. "Actually, I'm sorry how the whole week has gotten out of hand."

Red grimaced. "I've barely slept at all because I can't help but think that someone is out to get me."

Nick was right. Red had an impressive gift for hiding his anxieties from the public. To the guests, it appeared he'd taken the whole thing in stride—just another minor mess for the author of Trey Connor adventures.

"What are you reading there?" Red gestured to the book Faith carried.

"I belong to a book club, and we recently finished *The Blood of Sisters*."

Red peered at the cover. "Mystery, huh? Is it any good?"

"It's interesting," Faith answered. "Although I thought they took the blood type thing to an extreme."

"Nick tells me that fancy forensics is all the rage now."

"Well, it's more than that in this book. There's a lot of fascinating information about forensics and DNA testing, but it contains a whole section about how blood type supposedly can determine personality. I don't know that I buy into it."

Rufus found a stick along the path and picked it up, trotting alongside them with it in his mouth.

"You mean everybody with a certain blood type has a certain personality?" Red asked. "Like a horoscope?"

"That's the theory. For example, my blood type is A positive, and they say that makes me organized and a good listener."

Red studied her. "Well, you seem like those things to me."

"It also says I'm highly anxious and tend to bottle up my emotions until it takes a toll on me physically," Faith added.

Red laughed. "I take it you don't care for that assessment?"

"As a matter of fact, I don't."

They started up the circular drive that led to the manor's main entrance. The arc of sports cars was still parked on the lawn from last night. Canvas covers protected most of the vehicles from the salty air and morning dew. Angela's winning car appeared to be safely tucked back inside its gleaming trailer.

Red unclipped Rufus from his leash, grabbed the stick from the dog, and threw it across the lawn.

Rufus took off in a game of fetch.

"Now I have to know," Red said. "What does that book say about my blood type?"

"There's a chart in the back," Faith said, opening the book. "Which is yours?"

"It's not a common one," Red replied. "I'm B negative."

Scanning the chart, Faith said, "You're right. It says that only about 2 percent of the population has your type."

The author chuckled. "And here I'm always telling Nick I'm one in a million."

Rufus bounded over to Red and dropped the stick in front of him.

"So what does it say about my blood type?" Red asked as he tossed the stick again.

The dog barked and chased the stick.

She skimmed the list of characteristics. "You're strong-willed and goal oriented, and you'll fight for a cause you believe in."

"There you go," Red said. "That sounds complimentary."

"It also says you're prone to feeling like a failure, don't like being the center of attention, and stubbornly refuse to admit when you're wrong." Faith raised an eyebrow at the author.

"You're right," he said with a chuckle. "That book's full of nonsense. I'd just as soon crack open a fortune cookie or visit a palm reader if I want someone to make up things about my tendencies."

Faith laughed as she closed the book. "I'm with you there. The mystery is good, and the science is interesting, but I think only my doctor needs to concern himself with my blood type."

"True. I suppose I should thank you for some entertaining theories. Maybe I'll include some of that craziness in the next book." Red paused and stared at the ground. "I need to quit saying that."

Faith stopped and faced him. "Are you really retiring from writing altogether? Most writers I know say it's in their blood—no pun intended—and they couldn't stop even if they wanted to."

Red ran a hand through his hair. "Success is a funny thing. It never quite feels like you think it will."

Rufus presented his master with the stick once more.

Red tossed the stick much harder this time, grunting with satisfaction when it tumbled through the air and hit the side of Angela's car trailer.

The dog took off after the stick.

"The claws come out in everyone around you," Red went on. "You stop being a person or an artist, and you simply become an asset. A resource to be tapped. Or tapped out."

"That's so sad," Faith said genuinely.

"No, that's publishing," he muttered bitterly. "When you're number one, that means everyone else is out to take your spot."

A surprising surge of sympathy filled her. The man had boasted a successful career, and now he only wanted to enjoy his send-off. It was a shame that so many people seemed dead set against letting that happen.

"Oh, don't get me wrong," Red continued. "I'm grateful to have had such a good run. But I'm tired of glancing over my shoulder. I'll be happy to watch Trey drive his pretty Lamborghini off into the sunset when this last book comes out."

Rufus returned with the stick, and Red crouched down to give the dog an affectionate rub.

"It's a shame Nick doesn't want to let you do that," Faith said.

Red straightened up and studied her. "So you did hear my conversation with Nick," he said, tension filling his features.

"I'm afraid I did. Not that I meant to."

"Did you hear him threaten me?"

She'd heard an argument, yes, but would she classify it as a threat? "I heard you arguing."

"What else do you know?"

Faith felt it best to come clean. "I happened to see the manuscript in your briefcase before I returned it to you. I am sorry about that."

Red's face paled. "You opened my briefcase and read the manuscript?"

"No. I'd never do something like that. You left your briefcase in the library, and the papers spilled out when Watson knocked it off the chair." She remembered the word *terrible* scrawled in red ink across the bottom of the title page. "You seem awfully hard on yourself for such a talented writer. Please don't call your work terrible. I'm sure your fans would never agree."

Red seemed wounded by her words rather than complimented. *Vulnerable* would never have been an adjective she'd have used to describe Red Maxton before these past few days. At this moment, however, he appeared as small and uncertain as Stuart.

"That writing was private," Red blurted out, pacing. "It was never meant for public eyes. Not yours, not Nick's, not anyone's."

"I understand, and I'm sorry it happened," Faith said. "Please forgive me. And I'll mention it to no one. You have my word."

"No offense," Red told her, his gaze locked on the manor, "but I don't trust people's words anymore."

13

Faith poked her head into the kitchen. She needed to see a friendly face before meeting the challenge of the gadget exhibition that awaited her in the library.

Brooke removed a pan of blueberry muffins from the oven, then smiled when she saw Faith. "Good morning. You look like you could use a muffin."

"That sounds wonderful. Thank you."

Brooke slid a muffin onto a small plate and handed it to Faith. "What's up?"

"I had the strangest conversation with Red," Faith replied.

"I heard about his ex-wife's surprise appearance last night," Brooke said. "It sounds like Angela is a character and a half."

"Up until today, I might have said she was just as bold as Red. But he's frightened by what's happened, so maybe she's even bolder."

Brooke cocked her head. "Really?"

"It seems most of his public persona is only for show," Faith answered. "I think he's unhappy and feels threatened. It's sad. His life appears so glamorous from the outside."

Brooke tightened the knot on her apron. "Maybe espionage and intrigue aren't all they're cracked up to be."

"Maybe." After a pause, Faith ventured, "Have you seen Wolfe this morning?"

Brooke seemed to catch on to her hesitation instantly. "No. Why?"

"We had a bit of an argument last night." Faith went to the small table in the corner and sat down. "I wanted to go back to the cottage, and he wanted me to stay in the manor until this whole function was over. Turns out we were both right."

"What does that mean?" Brooke asked as she poured two cups of coffee.

"I was fine at the cottage, but I hardly slept for worry that I wouldn't be."

Brooke carried the cups to the table and sat down across from Faith. "Sometimes protective can feel a bit too protective, I suppose."

"I know Wolfe means well, but . . ." She let her voice trail off. It seemed pointless to get into it again. "We let the tension of the event get the better of us."

"Are you fighting?" Brooke took a sip of coffee.

Faith frowned. When Wolfe had left her cottage, he'd marched back across the lawn, irritation clear in every step. "More like we had a disagreement."

"So you are fighting. No wonder Diva and Bling wouldn't eat this morning."

"I hope not." Faith changed the subject by pointing out the official-looking paper pinned to the bulletin board beside them. The heading had caught her eye. "Garris really gave you a copy of our John Doe's forensic report?"

Brooke nodded. "I told the chief we found some of the stuff in our book to be a bit hard to believe, and he offered to show us what really happens in a small-town forensic investigation."

Faith took the paper off the bulletin board and scanned the different types of data. Some lines were redacted. After all, even unidentified bodies were entitled to their medical privacy. Most of the data involved columns of numbers with classifications she could hardly understand. Some were obvious, such as blood alcohol level, quantitative drug analysis, and wound or fingerprint processing. Others were so hard to decipher that they might as well have been in Latin.

One piece of data stuck out: John Doe's blood type. She wouldn't have given it much thought before this morning.

"This is from our John Doe in the hedge maze?" Faith asked again.

"Yes," Brooke replied. "Like I said. Maybe Garris was hoping we'd notice something he hadn't. He's frustrated that he still doesn't know who the guy is. I can't say I blame him. People shouldn't be able to drop off the radar like that in this day and age."

Faith stared at the page. "I don't know that I see something that Garris didn't, but I recently learned something he might not know."

Brooke leaned forward, obviously intrigued. "And that is?"

"Our John Doe has B negative blood," Faith responded. "If you remember from the book, only about 2 percent of the population has that type."

"So that narrows down the pool of who he could be, but it still doesn't identify him."

"Not unless you know that Red Maxton also has B negative blood."

Brooke's eyes widened. "How do you know that?"

Faith took a sip of coffee. "Red told me while we were talking. I mentioned the silly personality predictions in the back of *The Blood of Sisters*, and he asked me what the book said about him."

Peering at the report, Brooke said, "So our mystery body not only could be Red's clone, but he has Red's blood type."

Faith set her cup down. "They're related."

Brooke furrowed her eyebrows. "Can we say that for sure?"

"Well, no, not for sure. And even if they are related, that doesn't mean Red knows they are."

"Are you going to tell Garris?"

Faith gave the matter some thought. "I think I have to. It could be important if our victim is more than a doppelgänger. It must be part of the reason why he was killed."

"But who killed him?" Brooke asked. "Red's ex certainly sounds mean enough to do it. Maybe she thought the man was Red."

"Angela did threaten him. Nick said some things that made me think he suspects Stuart Everett." Faith sighed. "But I have to say, Nick is still the prime suspect in my eyes."

"Why?"

"I can't work it out yet," Faith admitted. "Nick desperately wants to continue the series, so maybe Nick thought he was actually killing Red, which would clear the way to continue the series without Red or the legal battle Red might put up." A chill ran down her spine at the thought. "Nick seems crafty enough to consider it."

"The cloth you found by Nick at the pool makes me think he's the one who threw the bricks through your windows," Brooke said. "He must have used it while he was painting the diamonds on them."

Faith frowned. "It does implicate him, but I think he's too smart to leave a sloppy clue like that. It doesn't quite add up."

"Could Nick and Angela be working together somehow?" Brooke suggested.

Now there was a partnership that really could send a chill down Faith's spine or make Red anxious. "It's possible. I expect Garris is checking into it. But there's something else that doesn't add up. Red's writing."

"What do you mean?" Brooke asked.

"I saw some of his work by mistake when Watson knocked it out of his briefcase in the library. It was a new Trey Connor manuscript."

"Wait. Hasn't Red been saying he's done with Trey Connor?"

Faith remembered the fear in Red's eyes. "He has. He got very anxious about the fact that I'd seen it."

Brooke frowned. "You have to tell Garris everything you know. It could be important to the case."

"I'll tell him about the blood type, but I still can't see any connection between the body and the manuscript," Faith said. "Part of the reason Red is retiring is that he wants his privacy. He wants what he writes to be his own business, not that of a lucrative franchise. Haven't you ever written something just for yourself?"

"I painted an ocean scene for Diva and Bling once," Brooke said. "You know, to put up against the back of their tank. But I don't think that's the same thing."

Faith thought of the little private book of poetry and personal musings tucked away in the drawer of her nightstand. How would she feel if someone she didn't even know well found it and read it? She might be as upset as Red.

"In any case, I'll wait until after the spy gadget exhibition to talk to Garris," Faith said as she finished her muffin. "They're displaying everything in the library, so I'm going to have Red and Nick in close proximity most of the afternoon. I'd rather not give either of them new reasons to be upset with me."

"Fair enough." Brooke pinned the forensic report on the bulletin board. "It's not as if our mystery hedge man is going anywhere."

It was bad enough the dog had ruined his morning walk, but now the cat found his library invaded by people unpacking crates of things that whirred, buzzed, clicked, and turned into other things. There were plenty of big, impressive rooms at the manor. Why ruin the peace of his sanctuary with a bunch of strange objects?

Normally, his human was happy when boxes of new things came to the library. She didn't enjoy boxes as much as any cat did, but the books inside made her smile. He liked seeing her happy.

But she wasn't happy this morning. That night at the manor had made for all kinds of intriguing explorations for him, but the cat was as relieved as she seemed to be to return to sleeping at the cottage.

Only going back home hadn't really helped. His human was still on edge. Even his long sessions of sitting on her lap and purring hadn't seemed to make her feel any better. She was on pins and needles this morning, and that wasn't good.

Somehow things grew more strained when the nice man came into the library. He had become a favorite of the cat and his person. This morning, the humans said ordinary things to each other in polite voices. But the cat was an intuitive creature, and he could tell things were not right.

They made too much of a show of oohing and aahing over the objects—"spy gadgets," the nice man called them. They may have thought they were fooling each other, but the cat could easily see tension between his human and the man who usually made her happy.

However, the cat had to admit that while the gadgets were intrusive, they were also fascinating. There were several electronic boxes with an entertaining collection of lights. He heard the humans talk about a dapper cane that opened to reveal a sword and a pair of wristwatches that sprouted tiny antennae to become two-way radios.

The cat's favorite was a fountain pen that uncapped to shine one of those fascinating red beams. The nice man flashed it around the room for him to chase. Even though it was undignified, the cat couldn't help himself, and he hunted the red light with wild abandon. His human should have one of these. Not only because it was great fun, but also because it made his human laugh and lightened things up between her and the nice man.

The red-haired man put a stop to the excitement when he came in. Why were humans so fond of saying, "Don't touch"?

Leave the humans to worry about the collection of strange gadgets. The cat could enjoy himself in the maze of empty boxes. Humans had the value of things mixed up sometimes. Boxes were wonderful things. Why did people discard them so quickly?

One box, however, seemed to get everyone upset. Why should an empty box upset them?

The cat leaped to a good vantage point in the balcony to see what the fuss was about.

"Where are the pressure cuffs?" Red demanded as he held up the empty box and shook it. "They're the centerpiece of the whole exhibition. Why aren't they here?"

"They were in the shipment from New York," Nick said. "I checked that list of items from the spy museum."

"Well, they couldn't very well have walked themselves out of the box on their own, could they?" Red snapped. "Where in the world are the cuffs? Did someone steal them to undermine me?"

"Calm down. They're probably just misplaced," Nick said as he rummaged through the pile of empty boxes and crates that had accumulated in the back of the library. "I'm sure we'll find them by the time the exhibition is slated to start. Everything else is accounted for."

"You don't misplace something like pressure cuffs." Red grabbed the shipping inventory from Faith's desk, then ran his finger down the list. He glanced at Wolfe. "You'd better not have some housekeeper hoping to make a quick buck by selling movie props."

"I assure you that I have every trust in the integrity of our full staff," Wolfe said evenly. "We often host events that deal with valuable merchandise, and our staff would never stoop to theft."

Red tossed the paper aside and began pacing. "So where are they?"

"What exactly are pressure cuffs?" Faith asked in an effort to defuse the rising tensions in the room.

"Doctor Vile's pressure cuffs. The main prop in one of the best scenes in any Trey Connor movie." Red stopped pacing and held up his two forearms. "These were actual working models of the prop used in the film. One of a kind. And now they're missing."

"Can you describe them so we know what to search for?" Faith asked.

Nick flipped through a nearby stack of papers with photos and descriptions, then showed them a photo when he reached the correct page. "They're silver wrist cuffs. They resemble a thick pair of mechanical handcuffs with a series of buttons on them. They're a movie prop."

"Only these aren't the prop version," Red interjected. "I had the spy museum send the actual working prototype built as a promotional experiment. The movie prop is plastic hype. These cuffs are the real thing."

"What do you mean by the real thing?" Wolfe peered over Faith's shoulder at the photograph.

"Exactly what the name implies," Nick explained. "Time-rigged cuffs designed to apply intense pressure after a specified countdown. When activated, they cut off circulation to the hands."

"They're extremely painful and dangerous," Red added. "Definitely not the kind of thing you want floating around unaccounted for."

Movie props were one thing, but who would actually create torture devices worthy of one of Trey Connor's evil nemeses?

Faith suddenly recalled Angela Gander's sinister threats, and she wondered if Angela had taken the cuffs. If so, she shivered at what Angela might be planning to do with them. Suddenly the collection of gadgets being gathered in her library felt more fearsome than fascinating.

"Of all the amazing devices that Trey Connor's ever used, why would anyone decide to make a functional pair of those cuffs?" Wolfe asked.

Nick and Red glared at each other.

"You said yes to the engineering school proposal," Red sneered.

"You brought them here," Nick replied.

"And you lost them."

"Gentlemen," Wolfe said, stepping between them, "can we agree that our focus right now should be on finding the cuffs? Given everything else that has happened this week, I think some caution is called for."

"I knew something like this would happen," Red muttered. "When did the boxes arrive?"

"Ms. Russell told me she signed for the delivery two days ago," Faith explained. "They've been in a locked storage closet until the staff brought them to the library this morning."

Red scanned the room. "And who was in here while you were unpacking the items?"

"The library hasn't been open to guests this morning," Faith said. "In addition to the four of us, the only other person who came inside was Mack. He delivered the display pedestals."

Red narrowed his eyes. "And you trust this Mack?"

"Absolutely," Wolfe cut in. "He's been with the manor for ages, and, as I told you, our staff is above reproach."

Red's eyes widened in alarm. "What if Angela is behind this?" he asked, his voice higher than it had been.

Faith had harbored the same thought. "She was here last night, and we don't know how long she was on the property before anyone figured out who she was."

"I wouldn't put it past that snake." Red started pacing again. "If anyone could find a way to slither into a locked closet, it would be her."

Faith noticed that Nick was very still and quiet. He'd acted surprised to see Angela last night, but she was starting to wonder if Nick was as skilled an actor as Red was. After all, someone must have let Angela in, and it could have easily been Nick.

"I don't see how," Wolfe said. "Only the executive staff has access to that storage closet. It's not as if she could have convinced anyone from housekeeping. The cuffs have to be somewhere in the library."

For the next hour, Faith, Wolfe, Red, and Nick turned the library upside down searching for the missing cuffs as they set up the rest of the exhibition. By the time the other gadgets had been positioned in their displays, Faith was beginning to despair of ever finding the cuffs.

The four of them stood around the pedestal in front of the library fireplace that had been designated for Dr. Vile's cuffs. The square glass cover stood over an empty pair of mannequin hands that had been sent to display the awful devices.

"We'll find them," Nick said hopefully. "They're not back at the spy museum, and they're not in our office in New York. The display hands made it, so the cuffs have to be here somewhere."

"If we don't find them by the time the exhibition opens, I'll move this pedestal out of sight," Faith said. "With all the other amazing pieces on display, maybe they won't be missed."

"Oh, they'll be missed," Red moaned. "Several people specifically told me last night that they were looking forward to viewing them."

"As a matter of fact, one of them was Denise," Nick said. "She made some comment about wanting to see what kind of torment you'd funded in the name of entertainment."

"I didn't fund them," Red countered. "The engineering department at my alma mater came to me with the idea as a contest. It was one of six fictional Trey Connor gadgets students were challenged to create in real life. I'm not some kind of monster commissioning weapons."

"Can you give us extra security?" Nick asked Wolfe. "We don't need any trouble tonight. Some studio executives are supposed to be here."

Red's expression morphed from anxiety to shock. "Movie guys? Why?"

"To pay tribute to you and the Trey Connor movies, of course," Nick answered.

Faith didn't miss the uneasiness in Nick's voice. She guessed it was more likely that the studio executives were here to try and convince Red to write three new books.

"You don't really expect me to believe that," Red replied. "I'm going up to my room to get away from all this nonsense. Then you can start practicing how to get along without me."

Faith watched Red exit the room. She really was coming to feel for the relentless pressure he was under. It seemed unfair to try and force the man to continue a career he wanted to retire from.

No wonder Red had been so disturbed when she'd come across his unfinished manuscript. If anyone knew he'd even attempted to write another story, they'd probably jump on it whether he approved or not.

14

Faith was glad to see Eileen's name come up on the screen of her phone. She answered, eager to hear her aunt's voice after such a tense time in the library.

"I just got back from a lunch date with a friend," Eileen said. "I've got something for you. Would you mind if I stopped by the manor?"

Faith glanced over at Wolfe, who was still getting an earful from Nick about the missing cuffs. Escaping the manor for a little while and talking over this new friction with Wolfe with Eileen seemed like an excellent idea.

"Actually, how about I meet you at the cottage?" Faith asked. "I could use a break from the library right about now."

"That sounds like I should stop at Snickerdoodles on my way over," Eileen said. "How have you been sleeping?"

The question seemed to double Faith's fatigue. "Not well."

"I've got something for that. But I'm still bringing goodies."

"I won't say no to either," Faith said, stifling a yawn.

"Sounds good," Eileen said. "I'll see you in twenty minutes."

Faith tried not to appear rushed as she grabbed her handbag and caught Watson's attention. Then she went over to Wolfe. "If it's all right with you, I need to step out for a bit. I'll return before the exhibition and search for the cuffs again."

"Of course," he replied, tension still in his voice.

"Come on, Watson," Faith called. "Back to the cottage with you."

She didn't care for the look Wolfe gave her at the mention of the cottage. Clearly, he still wasn't in favor of her being back there. She'd have to make him understand that the cottage was her home and she had no intention of running scared from it, even if she was still on edge and a pair of maniacal torture cuffs had gone missing.

As Faith crossed the Great Hall Gallery, she paused at the life-size statue of Dame Agatha Christie. "Did you have trouble convincing men you could take care of yourself?"

Agatha offered no wisdom on the subject, so Faith decided to take her cue from Watson. The cat always walked through Castleton Manor—through the world, in fact—as though his actions were dictated only by him. No one ever told Watson what to do. He loved Faith and accepted love from her, but she couldn't stop him from doing what he wanted to do.

As Midge often said, "No one ever owns a cat. You live with a cat, and a cat lives with you, but ownership never quite comes into it."

Two of the cover models from the contest stood admiring a portrait of one of Wolfe's ancestors that hung in the hallway.

"You've got to love a man with this kind of money," one of them said. "Wolfe Jaxon is single, you know."

Faith stopped walking and stepped back a little to put the statue between her and the women.

"Single, handsome, and wealthy," said the other woman. "Why do you think I'm sticking around? He's been to the Italian coast where I had that photo shoot last spring. I coaxed him into quite a conversation about good pesto and espresso."

"I thought you had your eye on that stockbroker in the city. The one with the house in the Hamptons."

"You should always keep your options open. And Wolfe Jaxon is a fine option."

"I heard that he has a thing with the librarian."

Now that was an interesting way to put it. Then again, Faith didn't really know what phrase she'd use to classify her relationship with Wolfe.

The other woman laughed with a tone so dismissive that Faith felt it sink down to the bottom of her stomach. "Librarian? Like that'll last. She's his employee. It's only a fling. Besides, who would want a plain old librarian when you could have me?"

It didn't matter that the woman had misread Wolfe's character by a mile. Faith was so exhausted, anxious, and annoyed that the model's words cut her deeply. On another day, she might have marched over and challenged the woman's shallow comments, but today wasn't that day.

Today it was all too easy to believe that Wolfe belonged out on the lawn with expensive sports cars and gorgeous models while Faith belonged in her tiny cottage with her books and her cat.

She chided herself for being ridiculous.

But as the pair of models sashayed away in a cloud of airy laughter, Faith couldn't quite make herself believe it.

"You don't believe that," Eileen said when Faith poured out her emotions the minute her aunt arrived at the cottage.

"I don't want to believe it," Faith said, ushering her aunt into the kitchen. She filled the kettle with the strong rooibos tea Eileen had brought and set the lid on to steep. "But we both know Wolfe and I come from different worlds."

Eileen had also brought a chamomile blend called Blackout that the shop owner had said could put a stallion to sleep, but now wasn't the time to try that brew. This afternoon called for both the strong tea and the espresso-laced tiramisu Eileen had picked up from Snickerdoodles.

"Those different worlds might matter to some other men of his pedigree, but you know Wolfe better than that," Eileen said.

"But the models are all so glamorous and beautiful."

"And you are strong, intelligent, and beautiful in a far deeper way." Eileen took Faith by the shoulders. "After all, would you ever say anything like that about someone? Even someone you didn't like?"

"Of course not." Faith felt a bit childish, as if she were pouting. "It's just plain mean."

Eileen took a seat at the table. "And you don't think Wolfe has seen enough of that kind of woman—even in his circles and maybe especially in his circles—to know exactly how cruel they are?"

"I suppose."

"Don't go doubting yourself or him," Eileen advised. "You're both scared."

"I'll tell you what I told Wolfe," Faith said, leaning against the counter. "I won't be scared away from my cottage."

Eileen smiled. "Come now. You're smart enough to know that most fights between people who care about each other aren't really about whatever they think they're fighting about."

Faith tried to untangle Eileen's complicated statement, but her brain was too weary. "What?"

"I know right now it feels to you like Wolfe is being . . ." Eileen paused, as if searching for the right word.

"Dominating," Faith finished for her. "Well, controlling, maybe," she amended.

"How about concerned?" Eileen suggested.

Faith set the two slices of rich layered cake on a pair of small plates and got out the teacups. She welcomed the sharp, strong scent that wafted up as she poured the tea. "He almost ordered me to continue staying at the manor."

"But he didn't order you. He ultimately let you make your own decision, though he made sure you knew how he felt about it. Would the arrogant Red Maxton have done that?"

"Red!" Faith nearly dropped the teapot. "With all the hullabaloo about the missing cuffs, I forgot to tell Chief Garris what I learned."

"What's that?"

Faith set the plates and teacups on a tray and carried it to the table. She sat down across from her aunt. "Red has the same rare blood type as our John Doe in the hedge."

Eileen's eyes widened. "How on earth did you find that out?"

Watson jumped onto Faith's lap and curled up.

Faith stroked the cat's fur as she told Eileen about her conversation with Red and the forensic report Brooke had received from the police department.

"Call the chief right now," Eileen urged. "In fact, use speakerphone. I want to hear what he thinks of a big clue like that."

Faith retrieved her phone and called Garris.

The chief listened to everything she had to say without uttering a word himself. When she was done, he concluded, "It's not much of a clue. It's not illegal to have a rare blood type. In fact, if they bear that much of a resemblance, it might even be more likely."

"But it means they're probably related, doesn't it?" Faith asked.

"It certainly makes it more possible," Garris responded. "But it doesn't give me the authority to get a warrant to swab Mr. Maxton's cheek for DNA testing."

"Could you ask Red if he's related to the man in the hedge?" Eileen chimed in. "Confront him with the blood type match?"

"Of course I could," the chief said. "But if Mr. Maxton hasn't offered the possibility, he probably doesn't know he has a relative matching this description."

"But if they have the same rare blood type—" Eileen persisted.

"Uncommon," Garris corrected. "That's not the same as rare."

"I'd call 2 percent rare," Faith argued. "And what are the odds of them looking identical and having the same blood type but not being related?"

"Remember this doesn't work like television," the chief said. "Even if I could convince a judge to give us a court order for a DNA test, it could take weeks, if not months, for definitive results. We could use cast-off DNA without needing permission, but it still wouldn't be speedy."

"What do you mean by cast-off DNA?" Faith asked.

"DNA from a drinking glass or a hairbrush," Garris answered.

Eileen turned to Faith. "We could get that."

"We could," Faith said. "It shouldn't be too hard to get a glass from the reception at this afternoon's gadget exhibition."

"Still, none of that places Mr. Maxton at the crime scene," the chief reminded them. "No, Mr. Westfield still tops my list of suspects. And I'm not ruling out Mr. Everett or Ms. Gander either. But if you learn anything else, please keep me informed." He hung up.

"Well, that was a bust," Faith grumbled as she set her phone down.

"You're letting the day get to you." Eileen picked up the tray and headed out toward the patio.

"It's been that kind of day." Faith sighed as she followed Eileen. "Days, actually."

As they settled into their chairs at the table, the pleasant scene reminded Faith of the lovely evening she'd spent in this same spot with Wolfe only two days ago. Watson even came outside and returned to his place on the stone wall that surrounded the small patio.

She gazed in the direction of the grand manor. Today the expansive lawn loomed like a huge chasm. She was so much more comfortable here in the humble cottage than in the enormous manor. Shouldn't that tell her something?

Eileen seemed to catch her thoughts, and she put a comforting hand on Faith's arm. "The first quarrel when you're in love is always hard."

Faith raised an eyebrow. Was she ready to use the word *love* where Wolfe was concerned?

"You don't really think this spat is about the cottage windows, do you?" Eileen's smile was tender. "You care deeply for him, and he's figuring out how much he cares about you. And that is very scary."

"He's being so . . ." A dozen frustrated words came to mind, but Faith chose to bite her tongue.

"Dominating? Controlling?" Eileen finished for her. "That's exactly how powerful men react when they're faced with fear. They're used to being able to bend situations to their will. Wolfe knows he can't do that with you, and it frightens him."

"I watch him with these other wealthy people, the way they welcome him as a peer and talk about cars and trips and empires. How can I be that?"

Eileen's face grew intent. "Faith Newberry, don't you dare let a snide comment by a foolish young model get to you. You don't *have* to be that. You don't have to be anything other than who you are to have a life with Wolfe. He's not looking for that from you or anyone else."

"But he was engaged to one of those world-class models once," Faith said. "I can't compete."

"And you don't have to." She tightened her grip on Faith's arm. "Come on now. This isn't like you. Shake it off and enjoy the relationship growing between you and Wolfe. It's been a long time coming."

Faith sighed. "I'm so exhausted lately. I feel like I haven't had a good night's sleep in weeks."

"The tea I brought is called Blackout for a reason. It will help."

"So would finding out whoever's been out to ruin Red's farewell party."

Eileen took a bite of tiramisu. "Do you agree with Garris that it's Nick?"

Faith wished she felt less foggy. It seemed too difficult to sort out this puzzle at the moment. "I'm more convinced that he was the one who threw those bricks through my windows. But why do that unless he's trying to scare me off from finding out something else?"

Eileen thought for a moment. "If Nick is so eager to get Red out of the way to continue the series with another author, do you think he shot whoever was in the hedge because he believed he was shooting Red?"

Faith leaned back in her chair. "That's the only theory that makes any sense to me now, but it has too many holes in it. Red wasn't expected that soon. Nick would have been sabotaging an expensive event, and he was in New York."

"Or he could have made it seem like he was in New York," Eileen suggested. "Or maybe he had a partner."

"Like Stuart or Angela."

"It's starting to sound like a plot right out of a Trey Connor novel, isn't it?" Eileen commented. "We'll need to get the whole book club mulling it over right away."

"Exactly." Faith felt the knots in her shoulders ease up a bit as she was reminded that she wouldn't have to solve this mystery on her own. "I'm glad you came by." She grabbed her aunt's hand. "I don't know what I'd do without you."

"Good thing you'll never have to find out."

When Faith and Watson returned to the manor for the exhibition, Wolfe, Red, and Nick were still inside the library. The atmosphere hadn't improved at all. In fact, the usually peaceful ambience of her beloved library was gone as she stepped into the room.

Red paced again. "This is out of control. Who has keys to this place?"

"A very limited number of the staff," Wolfe said.

His tone told Faith that he was near the end of his considerable patience. She'd evidently walked in on a conversation that had been going on the whole time she was gone. "Still no sign of the pressure cuffs?" she asked cautiously.

"Worse," Nick said. He pointed to the glass case with the mannequin hands they'd set up earlier.

Faith was shocked to see that one of the hands now held a three of diamonds playing card.

"I'm not going ahead with this party until I know how that card got there!" Red yelled. He seemed on the edge of hysteria—a far cry from the suave man Trey's creator needed to be in public.

"We all want to know that," Wolfe said, holding up one hand in a defensive gesture. "I've called Chief Garris to investigate."

"And we all know how useful that's been," Red scoffed. "I'm in real danger here. Forgive me if I don't put much faith in your two-bit small-town police department."

Something had to be done and quickly. Remembering that Olivia had brought the stunning rhinestone cuff bracelets she'd worn on her first Trey Connor cover, Faith made a proposal. "We'll need to put something in that case. Why don't I go upstairs and see if Olivia will lend us her bracelets from the first cover?"

"Fine," Nick agreed without enthusiasm. "I haven't got a better idea."

"The better idea is to find those cuffs," Red insisted. He scanned the library, then rushed over to a bookcase and started yanking books from the shelves.

"I'll be right back," Faith said. Glad to exit the tension-filled room, she made her way to the stairwell with Watson at her heels. On the second floor, she knocked on the door of the Daphne du Maurier Suite.

Olivia answered the door with some of her hair in hot rollers. "What can I do for you?"

Faith briefly explained the situation. "Would you mind if we borrowed your rhinestone bracelets to put in the display case?"

"What a delightful idea." Olivia opened the door and motioned her inside. "I planned to wear them with the gown that got shredded. At least now they'll get some attention after I lost the competition."

Faith walked into the suite with Watson following. "I thought you should have won."

"Well, thank you. But it doesn't matter much now, does it?" Olivia pointed to a pot of coffee and a pair of cups on the end table. "Red was up here earlier for coffee. He complained about the whole thing as if I could do something about it."

Faith stared at the cups. The cast-off DNA Garris needed had just landed in her lap. "I'll take the coffee cups downstairs for you when I go. It's no trouble."

Olivia regarded her for a moment. She was probably confused

by Faith's offer, as taking dirty dishes was not part of a librarian's job. Then she waved her hand toward the bureau. "You'll find the bracelets in the lower part of the makeup case over there. They're in the red velvet pouch."

"Thank you."

"Sorry, hon, but I need to finish my hair," Olivia called over her shoulder as she headed to the bathroom.

Faith went over to the dresser. Olivia's makeup case was fascinating. It was filled with bottles and compacts and beauty gadgets Faith had never seen. And the jewelry was amazing. It was like peeking into a glamorous lifestyle she'd never known. Sorting through the items, Faith felt like a little girl rooting through her mother's jewelry box to play dress up.

Olivia poked her head out of the bathroom. She held a curling iron in one hand and a cell phone in the other. "Did you find them?"

"Here they are." Faith spied the red pouch at the bottom. Opening the drawstring, she glimpsed the two stunning cuff bracelets. "Thank you. These will look fabulous in the display case."

"Good," Olivia said, then disappeared into the bathroom again.

Faith closed the pouch and turned to go, only to find Watson foraging in Olivia's suitcase on the closet floor.

"Rumpy!" she hissed. "Get out of there!"

Her warning had no effect as Watson continued pawing through the contents of the suitcase.

With a glance toward the half-shut bathroom door, Faith dashed over to the closet, ready to forcibly remove her cat from the room.

Then she saw that Watson had uncovered an old black-and-white photograph of a twelve-year-old boy with Red's features. What was Olivia doing with a snapshot of Red when he was a child?

Faith picked up the photograph and flipped it over. She gasped when she read the words *Rhett Maxton*.

Not Red, but Rhett. Another Maxton. Faith felt her pulse pound as she slipped the photo into her pocket and pulled Watson from the suitcase. "How do you do that?" she asked the cat in a whisper.

Carrying Watson, she grabbed a tissue from the bureau, then hurried over to the end table. She regarded the two coffee cups and used the tissue to pick up the one without a lipstick mark.

"Thanks so much, Olivia," Faith called, forcing a cheerful, casual tone into her voice. "I'll see you downstairs at the reception."

Olivia spoke, but the drone of a blow-dryer drowned out her words.

Faith made sure the door was latched behind her and rushed toward the back stairs. She needed to deposit these crucial pieces of evidence with Brooke or even Marlene until Garris arrived. She certainly couldn't stroll into the library with the photo and the coffee cup in her pocket.

She was descending the staircase when two hands slammed into her back. She fell forward as a scratchy blanket covered her head.

Watson yowled and hissed as he leaped from her arms.

When Faith took in a breath to scream, she heard the coffee cup shatter against the stairs before the world went black.

15

Faith woke to feel the damp cold of a concrete floor against her cheek. Her head throbbed, and the dim light of her surroundings made it hard to get her bearings. She was not in the manor, nor was she in the cottage. Through the fog of her growing awareness, she realized something was very, very wrong.

She went to touch the tender spot on her head and found she couldn't lift one hand without the other. Something hard and cold kept her hands together, her wrists close and confined. Slowly, minding her dizzying headache, she swung her legs around and shifted upright to sit against a nearby wall. The ribs of a corrugated steel sheet met her back.

As her eyes adjusted to the low slant of sunlight coming through one small and grimy window, Faith took stock of her surroundings. *What happened? Where am I?*

She didn't recognize anything about where she was. Judging by the crates, boxes, and tools strewn around, it seemed to be a shed. Cobwebs covered the shelves that rose from the dusty floor.

Faith squinted down at her wrists and gasped when she saw what held her hands together. The missing pressure cuffs that had been stolen from the exhibition were on her wrists, and a sinister blinking digital display read *4:08*.

Panic swept away her composure as Red's description of what the device would do leaped out of her memory. Why did anyone think it was a worthwhile endeavor to build a working set of these cuffs that were designed to cut off a person's circulation?

As she stared at the red digits, the display flashed and became *4:07*.

They're extremely painful and dangerous. Wasn't that what Red had said?

Faith wondered if the tiny, almost imperceptible change in the tightness of the cuffs was real or simply her imagination. After all, Red had never said if they slowly cut off circulation or clamped down all at once. Was one way any less horrible than the other?

Who had stolen the cuffs, and who had used them on her? Faith tried to think clearly, but logic seemed to dance out of her grasp.

Figuring out exactly where she was seemed to be the logical first step. If the manor was miles away, any hope of someone finding her before her fingers turned blue—or worse—was slim indeed.

Faith pushed her hair out of her eyes, glad not to see any blood on her fingers despite the nasty headache. Slowly, unsteadily, she grabbed the side of a nearby shelf and attempted to pull herself upright.

She couldn't stand all the way up because the shed was small with a low ceiling. She guessed the building was about the size of her bathroom in the cottage. Shelves lined every wall of the rectangular room, and a cement floor extended to all the corners. The single window was far too small to provide an exit.

The faint outline of a door could be seen on the opposite side. Faith threw herself at it, and she was disheartened but not surprised to find it locked. As she pushed on the door, she heard a rattling on the other side. Padlocked from the outside most likely. Faith was trapped inside the shed until someone let her out.

Trying not to allow the realization to make her panic even more, she focused on anything that could be considered a positive in this terrifying situation. As far as she could tell, she wasn't seriously injured. Also, she wasn't gagged.

Faith wasted no time. "Help!" she yelled as loudly as she could.

Only silence answered her.

She repeated the shout until she feared her voice would get hoarse.

Then Faith remembered her cell phone. She patted her pocket, hoping against hope that somehow she'd managed to put her phone in there. But she knew very well that it was sitting in her handbag in the library.

The phone wasn't magically in her pocket, and neither was the black-and-white photograph she'd slipped inside it before the world went dark. The sound of the coffee cup shattering jutted into her memory, and she knew the cup with Red's DNA was gone as well. The photograph was a crucial piece of evidence, and it had fallen out in the scuffle of her transport. Or it had been taken.

She thought she knew which one, but she didn't understand who would have snatched it.

It was possible Olivia had come out of the bathroom and seen Faith discover the photograph. Olivia was also the only one who could even suspect her of wanting to use Red's coffee cup as evidence. The model's list of grievances against the Trey Connor franchise certainly seemed to be growing. That meant Olivia could have been the one to abduct her, but it still didn't explain how or why.

If Faith had to credit anyone with enough malice to use these dreadful cuffs, it would be Angela. Had she managed to sneak back into the manor and do this? Angela's fight was with Red, not her, unless the photograph of Rhett Maxton was a threat to Angela. But how? Why?

Faith stopped her train of thought. None of that would matter unless she found a way to escape the shed. She had to figure out where she was.

She scanned the shed again, searching for some clue as to her location. Shovels, bags of seed, rakes, brooms, and other nondescript items told her she was in a storage shed but not which storage shed. Castleton Manor was a large estate, and she could hardly be familiar with all the many outbuildings on the grounds.

Of course, she might not still be on the manor grounds. Faith had no idea how long she'd been unconscious, so she couldn't even guess how far she'd traveled to wake up where she was.

The growing panic that raced up her spine only doubled when she glanced down at her wrists to see *3:51*. Less than four hours until the cuffs accomplished their dastardly mission.

Pushing aside several brooms and crates, Faith pressed her face against the filthy window. She couldn't see anything through it, so she used the edge of her shirt to try and wipe off the dirt. All it earned her was a grimy streak across her hem.

"Well, okay," she coached herself out loud. "It's time for drastic measures."

Grabbing the handle of one of the sturdier shovels, she aimed the point at the window and struck. It cracked.

"Progress," she announced to the empty air, scrambling for encouragement.

Another whack knocked out a corner of the small pane. In a few more whacks, the whole window was gone.

She threw down the shovel to peer out the window. She had hoped to recognize the view, but only overgrown shrubbery met her gaze. A rhododendron, with its broad, waxy leaves and fat pink blossoms, grew right up against the shed, explaining why so little daylight came into the small building. Whoever had hidden her here had chosen well.

Since Faith couldn't see anything to help her determine where she was, she used her other senses. While it seemed as if her pulse pounded in her ears, drowning out all other noises, she was able to make out the faint sound of waves. And when she tried, she could sort through the various smells in the shed to pick up the salty scent of an ocean breeze. She was near the coast, which meant she could still be near Castleton.

Encouraged, Faith craned her neck to see beyond the gnarly branches of the rhododendron. At first, nothing but clouds and sky came into view.

Finally, Faith recognized a pair of tall chimneys. "I'm still at the manor," she said with a prayer of thanksgiving. She was far from the mansion, but she had to be somewhere on the grounds.

That fact gave Faith new hope and determination. She turned around and scanned the shed for anything colorful that she could tie to the handle of one of the rakes and wave out the window.

It was awkward and difficult with her hands cuffed to each other, but she managed to take a yellow bag from a package of grass seed, poke a hole in it with the end of a rake, and find a piece of twine to tie it to a rake handle. It was ugly as flags went, but she hoped it would do the job if someone spotted it.

Faith waved her makeshift flag and yelled until her voice grew hoarse and the digits on her cuff read *3:11.*

No one noticed.

Discouraged, she slumped against the wall, fighting tears. It was the middle of summer, and the metal shed baked the air inside despite the newly "opened" window.

"Someone has to find me," she declared to the swirls of dust. The angle of the sunlight told her the sun was setting and night was coming. "They have to know I'm missing by now. I told Wolfe and Nick that I was coming right back with Olivia's bracelets." Swallowing hard, Faith flexed her wrists against the snug cuffs. She was sure they were tighter. "They'll come searching for me. I know they will."

She didn't know what time it was, but it didn't take much in the way of calculation to tell her it would be dark when the dreadful numbers ticked down to *0:00.*

Faith sat in the small patch of incoming sunlight, drinking it in as if she could save it up for the darker hours. She used the brightness to examine the cuffs. Could they really do the damage Red had threatened?

As she searched for a crack to widen or a seam she could pry open, she wondered if she could strike the cuffs against something hard like a shovel and damage the timing mechanism.

And what if she did somehow find a way to disarm them? She considered that they could be triggered to tighten instantly if she tried to destroy them. Anything and everything loomed in her mind as a threatening possibility.

If the cuffs had a seam or a hinge, it was out of her vision on the bottom. Unfortunately, the way her hands were bound side by side prevented her from maneuvering that part of the device into view. There was nothing in the shed that could be used as a mirror. If there was a weakness in the cuffs, she couldn't find it, much less figure out how to exploit it and gain her freedom.

"Where's Trey Connor when you need him?" she asked aloud with a bitter laugh.

The minutes ticked relentlessly by. Faith tried each of the walls, pushing against the metal panels in the hopes one of the rusted bolts would give way. None did.

She prayed as the last beam of sunlight left the shed, leaving the space in purple dusk that only lit fire to the slow burn of panic she'd been fighting. Someone must realize she was missing by now. She imagined Brooke's worried eyes, pictured Wolfe pacing the library while he talked to Chief Garris on the phone.

How many times had Wolfe warned her that her nose for mystery would lead her into serious trouble one of these days? How many times had she scoffed at his concerns and protective nature?

"I'll concede the point," Faith said to the darkening room. "You can be as right as you want for as long as you want if you'll only walk up to that door and unlock it."

Stealing a glimpse at the cuffs—with their lit digits that would mercilessly ensure she'd know exactly how much time was left no matter how dark the room became—she added, "Preferably in the next two hours and forty-two minutes."

She twisted her wrists inside the tightening cuffs, feeling the stronger friction against her skin. And then she saw something that made her jump up and rush to the window to catch the last of the light.

There, sticking out of one of the cuffs, was a hair.

A red hair.

It had to be Angela or Red.

"Did you take them yourself?" Faith accused Red out loud. But why would the author do it? Her intuition told her that wasn't nearly as likely as Angela working with Olivia. Faith pictured the vicious woman and her icy smile. "You did this to me!" The phone call she saw Olivia making must have been to Angela.

Olivia and Angela were working together. Did that mean the two of them had conspired to destroy the entire event? It wasn't much of a leap to imagine Angela tainting Nick's drink. There was certainly no love lost between those two. But Olivia making herself sick? Then again, wasn't that what models used the syrup for? And it would be simple enough to slash her own dress in a ploy to gain sympathy.

Was it possible that Angela was behind everything?

Faith ticked off the incidents and Angela's possible connection to them. Olivia could quite easily have drugged herself. Angela could have conspired with Olivia to slash the dress, and the gruesome pinning of the card to the pillow seemed quite in her character. If Stuart had been able to get onto the grounds, then Angela might have been able to as well—and framing Nick would certainly serve her purposes. Unless they were working together.

The possibilities seemed as endless as they were threatening. Had it been Angela who'd launched the bricks through her windows?

No one had known that Angela was at the manor before she burst into the reception. Which meant she could have been anywhere in the hours before and after the murder had taken place.

Faith concluded that Angela had to be guilty of some crimes if not all of them. Would Faith be seriously injured before she could tell anyone what she knew?

The only thing more aggravating than knowing Angela had made good on her threats, had taken the cuffs and used them on her, and was in league with Olivia was the fact that Faith could do absolutely nothing with the knowledge.

Letting her head fall back against the shed wall, Faith felt a tear slip down her cheek. She closed her eyes. When the timer ticked down to zero, she imagined it would hurt. Or maybe her hands would become more and more numb, and she wouldn't feel a thing. Maybe it—

Meow.

Faith opened her eyes. She sat very still, listening.

Meow.

"Watson!" she screamed, recognizing her cat's voice. "Watson, in here!"

She scrambled to the window, practically falling over in her rush to call Watson to her. With no mind for the jagged edges, she pushed her face as far out the window as the small space would allow.

There, at the base of the rhododendron's branches, sat her beloved Watson.

Faith practically burst into tears at the sight of her rescuer. "Come up here, boy!"

Midge, who as a veterinarian loved all animals but had a soft spot for dogs, especially her Chihuahua, had often joked that a cat would rarely come when called.

"Prove Midge wrong," Faith urged her cat. "Come on up here to me. I need you."

After a moment's consideration, Watson climbed the sturdy bush and leaped through the window into Faith's arms.

"Oh, Watson! Am I ever glad to see you." She hugged the cat so tight that he protested with a squeak.

After a few moments of the blissful reunion, it occurred to Faith that while Watson was welcome company, he wasn't exactly a solution to her predicament.

Or was he?

16

"I hate the idea of sending you away," Faith told Watson. "But I'll need you to get a message back to the manor. Now how are we going to do that?"

As quickly as she could before the light faded any more, Faith took stock again of everything in the shed, this time with a new purpose. Something in here had to identify the building she was trapped in. She forced herself to focus. Grass seed could likely be in multiple buildings. Rakes and shovels as well.

As she pushed aside a dusty box, her gaze landed on an old beekeeper's hood. "That's it, Watson," she declared, tugging the ragged hood from its spot on the shelf. While bees were no longer kept on the grounds, the abandoned hives stood in only one place on the far west side of the property. "That's where we are," she told the cat as she confirmed the angle of the sun's last rays.

Faith frowned. The stiff hood was almost as big as Watson. How could he ever manage to take it back to the manor? She spun around in a circle, grasping for ideas, trying not to peek at whatever numbers now appeared on her wrists.

Landing on a plan, Faith grabbed a burlap grass seed bag and rubbed it against the sharp edge of a shelf until it tore open. She poured out the seed and frayed the top quarter of the bag until she had enough string to close it and attach it to Watson's collar.

"Sorry about this. It's going to be a bit clumsy and uncomfortable." She stomped on the beekeeper's hood until it flattened enough to fold, then stuffed it into the grass seed bag. Maneuvering with two wrists bound together made the whole operation slow and difficult. But Faith had a way out now, and she would not stop fighting for her freedom.

"I'll help you out the window," she told Watson as she fixed the lumpy cargo to his collar. "Then you need to run back to the manor. Find Wolfe or Brooke or anyone you can." After a second, she added, "Except Angela or Olivia. Don't find one of them."

It might have been the fading light or her own desperation, but Faith could have sworn Watson nodded.

"Watson, what are you doing here?" the nice man asked.

The cat had finally succeeded in his mission. Not that it had been easy. The large bag with the stiff hood inside tangled on everything. It was heavy, slowing him down and dragging on his collar. But a cat of superior intelligence and bravery knew when the stakes were high. He did what needed to be done to help his person.

The nice man had been running all over the manor grounds searching for his human, forcing the cat to run everywhere in search of him. But the cat had persisted, knowing his cargo was only for someone intelligent enough to realize the message his human was sending, and that was the nice man.

He crouched down and studied the cat. "What do you have there? Did you get tangled up in something?"

Tangled up in a crime, *the cat wanted to howl, but he merely pulled the bag toward the man's feet.*

"Who tied this to you?"

The cat stared at him, willing him to understand.

Realization shone on the nice man's features. "Did Faith send you with this?" He immediately untied the scratchy bag and took out the large hood. "What is this?"

It's where she is! I tried to stop it, but she's out there. Go get her! *The cat pawed at the hood, pushing it closer to the nice man. He meowed as insistently as he could.*

"Mack," the nice man called to the older man a few yards away, "come look at this."

"Watson, my boy, what did you bring us?" The older man squinted at the hood.

There were two of them now. Surely one of them would reason out the clue he had worked so hard to deliver.

"That's a beekeeper's hood, isn't it?" the nice man asked.

The old man nodded as he examined the hood. "We used to have bees, remember?"

They were wasting precious time. The cat meowed louder and batted at the hood again to tell them to hurry up.

"I remember," the nice man said.

"We kept the bees on the far west side of the property."

"What's there now?"

"Nothing but an old shed and empty hives."

Finally, after what felt like forever, the nice man's eyes lit up. "A shed. What if Faith is trying to tell us that's where she is?" He grabbed the hood and jumped inside the little cart the old man drove around the manor.

"Why on earth would she go there?"

"She's missing. Someone took her there. She could be in danger. She sent Watson back to tell us where she is."

"Let's go." The old man climbed into the driver's seat of the cart.

The nice man leaned down and gave the cat a vigorous pet. "Good boy, Watson. You're a hero tonight."

The cat jumped into the cart before it set off. He'd done it. He'd saved his human when she needed him most. Of course, he'd always known himself capable of it—all cats are born heroes—but now everyone at the manor would know it as well.

Time dragged on with a sinister slowness. Every bit of light that left the sky seemed to take more of Faith's courage with it. Eventually, as the last of the light abandoned the shed, Faith fell into moans of fear and worry. Finally, she simply closed her eyes and tried to make peace with the dark silence.

"Faith!"

At first, Faith thought she'd imagined the shout that startled her out of her daze. Then she opened her eyes to see a flicker of a flashlight beam bounce through the broken window.

Her whole body snapped to attention as she heard Wolfe's voice call again, "Faith!"

As she scrambled to her feet, relief rushed through her with such force that she lost her balance and almost fell. She staggered over to the door. "In here!" she yelled in return. "I'm in here!"

"The door's on the other side," Mack said.

She heard the rattle of tools and the engine of the little vehicle Mack used to traverse the large estate.

She'd never been so overjoyed to hear the clink of keys as Mack found the one he needed for the padlock. The old hinges creaked as the door swung open. Then a flashlight pierced the darkness of the shed, practically blinding Faith.

"Faith!" Wolfe's eyes were wide with alarm, his voice breathless as if he'd run the entire length of the estate.

"Wolfe!" Faith stumbled toward him, her knees giving out.

He caught her and held her tight for a second, then pulled back to view the cuffs.

Faith glanced down. The numbers announced *1:26* left before they triggered.

"Are those the pressure cuffs?" Wolfe asked, his voice nearly hoarse with shock.

"Yes. The working ones. Get them off me. Please." Even though it appeared that they had more than an hour to defuse the cuffs, she couldn't stand the thought of them touching her for one more minute.

Wolfe turned to the maintenance man. "Mack?"

Mack, who'd come in with Watson close on his heels, examined the device for a moment. "Gotta break them."

"How do we do that without breaking her wrists?" Wolfe asked, glancing around the shed.

"I was wondering that myself," Faith replied.

"I'll find something." Mack began rummaging through the supplies.

"Watson found you?" Faith asked Wolfe.

He nodded. "Remind me to give this cat a raise. Or a medal. Or a lifetime supply of tunaroons."

Watson twined around Wolfe's legs, purring.

"He is clever," Mack said as he picked up a garden trowel and the larger shovel Faith had used to break the window. "But it was you who gave us the best clue. Only one building on the grounds is anywhere near the old beehives."

Wolfe's expression darkened. "Who did this to you?"

"At first I didn't know. Someone came up behind me in the stairwell and threw a blanket over my head. That's the last thing I remember. But I'm sure it was Angela."

"Angela?" Wolfe said, disbelief in his tone. "She's still here? She did this?"

"Watson discovered a photo of a boy who looked identical to Red. The writing on the back said his name is Rhett Maxton. It was in Olivia's room, and that's where I was coming from when . . ." Faith raised the hideous cuffs in explanation.

Wolfe gaped at her. "Are you saying Red is related to the man we found in the hedge?"

"He has to be. The resemblance is uncanny, and he has the same last name. But why would Angela want to hurt me?"

"Let's deal with that later," Mack advised, upending a crate.

"Right now, wrap this sack around your hands and put your arms down on the crate."

"Don't hurt her," Wolfe cautioned.

"I'm not planning to," Mack replied. "But it's going to take a little doing to get this right."

"Maybe we should drive her to the police department or the hospital," Wolfe suggested.

"I can't wait that long," Faith said as she followed Mack's directions. "I need them off now."

Mack eyed the cuffs again, paying particular attention to the thin stretch of metal between the two cuffs where the digits blinked. He carefully positioned the point of the trowel right in the middle of the stretch. "Hold the flashlight on that," he directed Wolfe. "And hold the trowel right there with your other hand."

"Are you sure this won't hurt her?" Wolfe asked as he took the flashlight from Mack.

"Just do it," Faith pleaded as the display flashed another minute gone.

"Stretch out your fingers," Mack advised. "Don't make a fist."

Tense as she was, Faith told her hands to relax, wiggling her fingers under the sack wrapped over her hands.

"Both of you look away in case pieces go flying," Mack said, his voice steady. He raised the heavy shovel over his head, ready to bring it down on the sharp trowel. "Ready?"

Faith took a calming breath, closed her eyes, and prayed. "Ready," she said.

The blow of the shovel radiated through her wrists. It was startling, but it didn't hurt her.

She opened her eyes to see Mack bending over a small crack in the cuffs. "Do it again," she said to Mack.

"I'll do it as many times as it takes to break these things," Mack said.

"Be careful," Wolfe cautioned.

Once again, Mack brought the shovel down to hit the trowel, and this time an audible crack greeted the impact.

"Twist your wrists a bit," Mack instructed.

Faith did so, and she was relieved to feel the cuffs starting to give. The display blinked for a moment.

"It's working," Wolfe said.

After another mighty blow, the countdown display finally went dark and the cuffs separated. For a split second, Faith expected the trigger to go off and for the individual cuffs to tighten over her wrists in some sort of trap, but no such thing happened.

"You're safe," Wolfe said.

"Get them off, Mack," Faith implored.

Wolfe took one of her arms and pointed the flashlight all around the cuff. "There's a seam on the bottom."

The cuffs were still tight, and it took some effort to twist them around Faith's wrist until the seam was on the top, but once achieved, Faith placed her arm on the crate again and motioned for Mack to continue.

"We'll need to be a bit gentler with this bit," Mack said, picking up a brick from the shed floor. As Wolfe held the light, he hammered and twisted and pried until the silver circle split open.

Faith yanked her hand out with a cry of relief.

Mack made short work of the other cuff.

When she was finally free, she rubbed her wrists to get her circulation going again, then hugged Mack. "I don't know how I can ever thank you enough."

"No need. I was glad to get them off."

Watson sat down next to her and purred.

Faith scooped up the cat and cradled him. "I don't know how I can ever thank you enough either."

Watson purred louder.

She checked her hands and wrists for injury. Her wrists were red and rubbed raw, but other than that, she seemed to be unharmed.

Faith could practically see Wolfe wrestling his anxiety under control. He embraced her. "Why didn't you stay at the manor when I asked? This wouldn't have happened if you'd been under my roof."

Faith didn't think that was true. In fact, she'd been abducted from under Castleton's roof. This would have happened no matter where she'd been sleeping. But it hardly seemed the time to split those hairs. She offered no answer but simply let herself lean against Wolfe. Now that she was safe, a sudden exhaustion pulled her down.

"I'm so thankful you're all right," Wolfe said as he circled his arms more tightly around her. "When we discovered you were missing, I was terrified."

"I wasn't exactly calm myself," she said. Suddenly all the reasons why they'd squabbled seemed silly and unimportant. "Thank you for finding me."

"Watson deserves the credit," Wolfe said, petting the cat. "But why on earth would Angela need to silence you for finding that photo?"

"I don't know." She leaned back and met his gaze. "But I'll bet Olivia does."

17

"Olivia?" Wolfe asked.

"I'm sure Angela and Olivia are working together," Faith explained, holding Watson tightly to her chest. "While I was getting Olivia's bracelets, she was drying her hair in the bathroom. She had her cell phone with her, so she must have called Angela when she realized I discovered the photo and was taking the cup."

Wolfe frowned. "What cup?"

"I was carrying a coffee cup Olivia said Red had used. I was going to give it to Garris for DNA evidence so we could prove Red's relationship to the body. But it broke when Angela attacked me." Faith raised one hand to the side of her head where it still throbbed.

"Let's return to the manor." Wolfe ushered Faith outside and helped her into the back seat of the cart. Then he climbed in beside her.

Mack got behind the wheel, started the cart, and headed toward the manor.

"Are you sure Olivia called Angela?" Wolfe asked. "I thought she already took her car and left town."

"That's what she wants you to think," Faith countered. "But you're right. She could have called Nick. We don't know who she's working with. She might even be working with both of them."

"Nick did take a call and leave the library after you did," Wolfe said. "I figured it was the spy museum. And he was very late coming back to the exhibit."

"What I still can't figure out is why," Faith mused. "Believe me, I've had a lot of time to think about it, and I can't work out how all the pieces fit together."

"The photo must be the key," Wolfe said. "Where is it now?"

"Gone, of course." Faith sighed with frustration. "Which means I can't prove what I know. And we don't know where Angela is."

"We'll find her," Wolfe promised. "She tried to hurt you, and she almost succeeded. That's crime enough."

"But we don't have any proof," Faith reminded him. "I don't have the photograph. I can't even prove it was Angela who cuffed me unless we get the red hair I found analyzed for DNA, and that takes too long."

"I've got the cuffs," Mack said, holding up a bag with the broken pieces. "Maybe there's fingerprints on them. That's faster, isn't it?"

"I doubt those prints are any good after what we've done to the cuffs," Faith said. "And even if I could prove Angela cuffed me, that doesn't confirm she's the murderer." Fright and fatigue began to make her feel helpless. Angela couldn't get away with this. They had to do something to prove the horrible thing she'd done.

"We need to confront Red about the photo. Clearly, he knows more than he's telling. And Olivia." Wolfe took Faith's hand. "What would have happened if we hadn't found you in time?"

"I don't know," Faith admitted. "I'm not sure I want to know."

Watson snuggled against his mistress.

Wolfe gave Faith a long, concerned look before pulling out his cell phone. "Garris is here searching for you. I'll ask him to put out a bulletin for Angela and take Olivia into custody this minute."

Faith nodded.

Wolfe dialed the chief. "We found Faith. Angela Gander put the pressure cuffs on her. With help from Olivia. We had to break them off Faith's wrists before something awful happened."

As Wolfe listened to Garris's response, surprise washed over his face. "What? You're sure?" He turned to Faith and said, "Angela Gander and her broker have been arrested at the New York border for auto theft. Evidently, that prizewinning Jaguar didn't come to her by legal means."

"So Angela's not here?" Faith asked.

Wolfe shook his head.

Faith gasped when she realized there was only one other person with red hair at Castleton tonight.

And he had a lot of explaining to do.

"Are you out of your mind?" Red shouted.

Chief Garris had sequestered Red in the salon to question him about the kidnapping and the pressure cuffs. Faith and Wolfe watched the interrogation as they all waited for Officer Tobin to get Nick and Olivia.

"I don't know where those cuffs went to," Red continued. "I wanted them found. I was horrified they were lost."

"So you deny you put those cuffs on Miss Newberry and locked her in that shed?" Garris asked. "I won't find your fingerprints on the cuffs when I dust them?"

Red wheeled and faced the police chief. "Why would I use cuffs I need to hurt a woman I hardly know and lock her in a shed I don't have keys for? I don't even know where that shed is." His voice gained volume with every word. The frightened man Faith had seen in the library was fast transforming into an angry, forceful one.

Garris folded his arms. "As a matter of fact, that's exactly what I'm asking you."

Faith gathered her courage and stepped between them, staring up at Red as if the inches he had over her in height didn't matter one whit. Then she asked him the question on which everything hinged. "Who is Rhett Maxton?"

Red didn't reply.

"I'm sure you're aware that I found a photograph in Olivia's room," Faith said. "It's a picture of a boy who looks just like you. And the back of the photo identified him as Rhett Maxton. Who is he?"

"You know exactly who was found in our hedge maze," Wolfe added. "And you had to silence Faith when she discovered the photograph that proves it."

"Only a small percentage of people have B negative blood," Faith continued. "You do, and so does the body in the maze. You can't hide it any longer."

Red threw his hands up in the air. "I don't care who's in your hedge maze and whether he resembles me or not."

The door to the salon opened, and Officer Tobin walked in with Olivia. "Ms. Bishop, as requested. Mr. Westfield is on his way."

Olivia glanced warily around the room. "What's going on?"

"Ms. Bishop, is there a photograph missing from your possession?" the chief asked.

Olivia attempted to remain calm, but she clenched one of her fists. She didn't answer the question.

Garris cleared his throat and raised his eyebrow. Faith knew she wouldn't have been able to remain silent under his formidable glower.

Finally, Olivia swallowed and said, "It's not actually my photograph. I was keeping it for Red."

"You stole it from me," Red corrected, then suddenly grew silent as he realized his slip.

"A woman in my position needs leverage," Olivia said. "Not that it got me the cover I was hoping for, did it, Red? My little bit of assistance here was supposed to fix that, but I see it hasn't."

"We were never on the same side," Red muttered.

"Not anymore, obviously," Olivia sneered. "Besides, the photograph's not really missing because I saw Faith take it. What did you have to promise her to get it back, Red? Your Lamborghini?"

"He used other persuasion, I'm afraid," the chief said as he walked over to a table. He picked up a bag, then removed the pieces of the broken pressure cuffs and held them up.

Olivia had the decency to appear shocked as she stared at Red. "You had them all along? And you used them? Now who's the vile one?"

Garris set the cuffs on the table. "Who is Rhett Maxton?" he asked Olivia.

"Livie," Red growled at the model.

Olivia lifted her chin. "Rhett Maxton is Red's twin brother."

"I want to make sure we're all very clear on this, Ms. Bishop." The chief's voice took on an especially official tone. "You are stating that the photograph Miss Newberry removed from your room is the same one you stole from Mr. Maxton. And that photograph is of Red's twin brother, Rhett."

"Yes," she said evenly.

"Where is that photograph now?" Garris asked.

"Judging by Red's expression, I'd say that she has it," Olivia said, motioning to Faith. "Do you have my bracelets too? They never did show up at the exhibition."

"That's because Red kidnapped me right after you warned him that I'd found out about his brother," Faith retorted. "He must have taken the photo and the bracelets."

The chief addressed Olivia. "You knew Red had an identical twin, and you didn't think that was important information given the body we found?"

"It's not my secret to tell," Olivia declared. "You don't get a long career in my business without learning when to keep your mouth shut. It's best to hang on to leverage like that. You never know when you might need it."

Garris took a step toward Olivia. "In the middle of a murder investigation is not the time to keep your mouth shut or play your odds."

Olivia narrowed her eyes at him but remained silent.

"And how is it you came to know so many unpublicized details about the Maxton family?" the chief persisted.

Olivia smirked. "Perhaps you should ask Red why his marriage to Angela went up in smoke."

Faith glanced between Red and Olivia. "You two?"

Olivia seemed to take Faith's surprise as an insult. "Is that so hard to believe?"

"Your history with Red would explain why Angela said she'd do anything to keep you off the cover of the final book," Faith said.

Nick burst into the room. "What's going on here?"

"Angela and her broker have been arrested for auto theft," Faith answered. "You've lost your cover car." *And I suspect a lot more than that*, she thought. After all, a stolen car was the least of tonight's problems.

Nick gaped. "Angela stole that car?"

"Forgive me if I'm not surprised," Red snapped.

"Was she the one who damaged the other cars?" Nick asked.

Red pointed at Nick. "So quick to pin it on her, are you?"

"It was Red who stole the cuffs and used them on me," Faith declared to the editor, watching his reaction. Did he already know this? Had he been part of the plot?

"He what?" Nick appeared genuinely stupefied for a moment. Then he turned and glared at Red. "Did you drug me?"

"I can't say I didn't enjoy that little episode," Red replied, his voice gaining more power and growing darker. "But I had Denise's help with that." He gave Olivia a smug smile. "She drugged you too."

"You little weasel," Olivia hissed. "And to think I helped you by tipping you off about the photo."

"Helped? More like double-crossed me, you mean," Red shot back. "I knew you were never on my side. Denise wanted that cover badly, so she was quite cooperative to gain my vote. The bit with the dress was her idea, but I liked the drama of it."

"Speaking of double-crossing," Olivia said. "How did she get into my room?"

"She borrowed a key. Neither one of you knew I was working with the other," Red bragged. "It was a complicated situation but very satisfying. And easier than I'd thought, given my practice juggling you and Angela."

"Red, what's going on?" Nick asked, raising his voice. "What have you done?"

Garris held up a hand. "I'm going to ask you this nice and clear, Mr. Maxton. Is the man we found in the Castleton hedge maze your twin brother, Rhett?"

"What?" Nick stared at the author.

Unless Nick was a great actor, it seemed as though he wasn't aware of Red's brother. Faith began to wonder just how far this tangle of secrets went.

"How should I know?" Red shouted. "We don't talk. He's emotionally unstable. Actually, he's outright crazy. I cut ties with him years ago. Luckily with someone that greedy, a hefty settlement and a nondisclosure agreement go a long way."

"Twin?" Nick seemed to be scrambling to put the facts together.

Wolfe glared at Red. "I don't believe that. You know exactly where Rhett is, and that's why you tried to hurt Faith."

"Even if that man is Rhett—and I'm not saying he is, not by a long shot—that doesn't mean I killed him," Red argued.

"But it does make you highly suspicious for hiding it," Wolfe said.

"Oh no," Nick moaned, realization dawning on his features.

"You don't need a DNA test to prove it's Rhett. All you have to do is peek under Red's left arm," Olivia offered, her tone icy as she sneered at Red. "You both have them, don't you?"

Red's expression darkened even more. "You're enjoying this too much, Livie."

The elegant woman hardened her eyes. "I'm not enjoying it at all. It doesn't feel a bit like the victory lap I wanted."

"What are you talking about?" the chief asked Olivia.

"Red has a diamond-shaped birthmark under his left arm," Olivia explained. "That symbol doesn't only show up in his novels. If your dead body has one, it's Rhett."

"The coroner's report mentions the same birthmark," Garris confirmed. He nodded at Red. "Let's see it."

With obvious reluctance, the author unbuttoned his shirt, slid his arm from the sleeve, and raised it to reveal a reddish-brown diamond-shaped birthmark. Then he swiftly pushed his arm back through the sleeve and redid the buttons.

"Now you know where the idea for Trey's calling card came from," Olivia announced.

"I always wondered how you came up with that," Nick said.

Faith pondered what had happened in Red's family. What would it take for a man to disavow his twin brother and wipe him completely from his life the way Red had?

"They were actually very much alike," Olivia mused. "Handsome and shy. But once Red figured out who he could be with a little imagination—well, there really wasn't any comparison."

Given Red's public and private personalities, it wasn't hard to see how friction might arise between the brothers. One shy twin found a way to conquer the world while the other struggled.

Olivia gave Red a bitter look. "I know you hated Rhett and you did your best to ignore him, but I can't imagine that even you could be capable of killing him."

"Did you murder your brother?" Garris asked gravely.

Red failed to reply.

"What made you murder Rhett Maxton?" the chief pressed.

Red pointed to Nick. "He made me do it."

18

"**M**e?" Nick blurted out. "I did no such thing."

Red crossed his arms over his chest. "You really think I didn't know what you were doing? What you, Stuart, and Rhett were plotting? What do you take me for?"

"Stuart and..." Nick sank into a chair and hung his head. "Stuart's mystery author was your brother. I didn't know. I didn't even know you had a twin brother. How do you hide something like that for so long?"

"So now you're pretending like you didn't know," Red sneered. "Like Rhett wasn't the easy solution to all your problems." He waved dismissively. "Keep your day job. You're a terrible actor."

"I swear I didn't know. I mean, I was working with Stuart to groom an author. But Stuart wouldn't tell me who it was. He only told me that I'd be blown away by the author when he finally revealed his identity." Shock washed over Nick's face. "I told Stuart he had to produce someone just like you. And he did. No wonder Stuart boasted."

"He was going to produce Rhett," Faith said. "But Rhett was murdered before Stuart could introduce him to you."

"And Stuart is the genius you were going to let take over the Trey Connor series?" Red snarled.

"I paid Stuart well for absolute secrecy," Nick said. "How did you find out?"

"Because like I said, Rhett is a greedy idiot," Red replied. "He got peeved when you rejected his first draft with Stuart. So he came straight to me, shoved his so-called brilliant manuscript in my face, and crowed about how he'd won. How you were totally behind him, how you were getting ready to let him take over Trey Connor whether I wanted it or not."

"The manuscript I saw," Faith said, realizing the author had only been listed as *R. Maxton*.

"That was Rhett's." Red glared at Nick. "Stuart's a terrible book doctor and an even worse author. I can't believe you think so little of Trey that you'd hand him over to a hack like that."

"Why didn't you confront Nick with what you knew?" Wolfe asked.

Red laughed darkly. "And tip him off that I knew his scheme? Let him weasel out of it behind the scenes?" He turned to Nick. "No sir. I was going to find a way to make you fall flat on your face in disgrace in front of all my fans."

"So you slashed the tires and made sure everyone thought it was me." After a moment, Nick added, "The drink? The bricks?"

"Denise came up with the idea for the drinks," Red admitted. "As for the cars, I have to believe that was Angela's doing. I'd never harm a car. Except for hers, that is."

"But you smashed my windows and put those horrible cuffs on me?" Faith demanded.

"Some people are too nosy for their own good," Red replied.

Faith couldn't believe how nonchalant Red seemed about his actions.

"Trey Connor is mine," Red declared. "I created him, and I gave him the charisma that sold all those books. Me. It's not a hand-me-down for Rhett to wear, and it's definitely not my idea of a family heirloom. I get to finish my career on my terms, not Nick's, Stuart's, or Rhett's. Why do you think I asked Rhett to come here? I wanted to tell him face-to-face so there'd be no misunderstanding. I wanted him to see my eyes when I told him Trey could never be his."

"You wanted to see his eyes when you shot him," Garris interjected.

"Rhett always let things get out of hand," Red went on, ignoring the chief's statement. The author's hands flew in huge gestures as he talked. "Never backed down or shut up or knew when to quit. He's nothing like me. Nothing! He's a stupid, weak little man who won't hear no. The gun was supposed to show him I meant business. But there was only one way to shut him up."

A stunned silence filled the room.

Then Red continued. "When he pulled one of my three of diamonds cards out of his pocket to show me how good it looked in his hands, I told him it would look better on his dead body. And I shot him."

Faith winced.

Olivia put a hand to her chest. "How could you?"

"Oh, don't act so shocked," Red snapped. "I don't regret it. I hated him. I'd rather see him dead than let him have Trey, and he'd never stop trying to get him. And Nick was going to sit there and let him muck up my legacy."

"But you've done that yourself," Nick said, his voice thick with shock. "You killed Trey when you killed Rhett. It's over now."

"If I know you, you'll find a way to spin this into more PR," Red grumbled.

"No," Nick said, sinking back into his seat. "Not this."

Garris pulled out his handcuffs. "These aren't spy gadgets, but I'm convinced they'll do the job. Red Maxton, I'm placing you under arrest for the murder of Rhett Maxton, property damage to Castleton Manor, and aggravated assault of Faith Newberry. And probably a few other things by the time we're done here. Let's go."

Faith, Brooke, Midge, and Eileen—along with Watson and Atticus—sat in their regular meeting place in the Candle House Library the next morning.

Faith recounted the wild story of being imprisoned in the shed with the pressure cuffs, followed by Red's murder confession.

"It was his twin brother, not a look-alike impersonator," Midge marveled. "I'm surprised one of us didn't think of that."

Eileen stopped her knitting. "Who would suspect a man of hiding and then killing his twin brother?"

"The same man who slapped a pair of cuffs on Faith designed to cut off her hands, that's who," Brooke scoffed.

"Cut off circulation, not cut them off." Faith glanced down at her wrists. "At least I hope. I don't actually know what would have happened if they'd been allowed to fully activate."

"Nothing good," Brooke said warily.

"Thank goodness for Watson," Midge said. "He's a hero."

The cat meowed as if he agreed.

"So Red killed Rhett," Brooke said. "What about Olivia?"

"She's guilty of tipping off Red that I had the photo and of hiding what she knew about Rhett," Faith responded. "But I'm not sure she can be charged with any of those as a crime. It's not obstruction if you weren't questioned in the first place. As for Denise, on the other hand, her next cover shoot might involve an orange jumpsuit."

"And that Stuart fellow. What do you suppose will happen to him?" Midge asked. "If he was working with Rhett, how did he not know the man was dead in the hedge maze?"

"Garris brought him in for questioning, and it turns out the two had never met," Faith explained. "They found each other on a Trey Connor fan site and worked up the scheme over e-mail when Red announced his retirement. Stuart thought revealing that his mystery partner was really Red's brother would be the key to closing the deal."

Brooke snorted. "As if that would actually work. You're seriously telling me Stuart knew he was working with Red Maxton's brother but not that Rhett was here in Lighthouse Bay? It's crazy."

"Crazy or not, I expect Stuart's career is as finished as Red's," Faith said.

"Why?" Midge asked. "He may not have been clever in how he

went about it, but he didn't do anything wrong. He was doing the job Nick agreed for him to do."

"And using that against Red. Who ended up a murderer, which proves my point. It's crazy." Brooke checked her watch. "I'd better get back to the manor. No matter how intense a mystery gets, people still need to eat."

"Atticus and I need to go too," Midge said. "We have to swing by the bakery."

Midge and Brooke left, but Eileen held Faith back. "Can you stay for a minute? I want to ask you something."

"Sure," Faith said.

"That was quite an ordeal you had," Eileen began.

"The whole Trey Connor debacle was a little dramatic, wasn't it?"

Eileen crossed her arms. "That's not what I meant. You were in real danger. If Watson hadn't reached Wolfe—"

"Don't do that," Faith interrupted her gently. "We don't really know if the cuffs would have done what they were supposed to do. Or what the damage might have been. I'm safe now, and that's what I prefer to focus on."

"What does Wolfe think about what happened?" Eileen asked. "You told me he was quite emotional when he found you."

"I suppose it was an ordeal for both of us," Faith answered.

Eileen raised an eyebrow. "Suppose?"

"Since the confrontation with Red, Wolfe has been holed up in his office." She paused before adding, "I haven't really seen him."

"That's odd, don't you think?"

"The man does have a business to run. And an event that seems to be requiring everyone's full attention." That was what Faith had been telling herself, but Eileen could probably see how little she believed it.

Wolfe had held her tightly after the cuffs were released and all the way back to the manor that night. But it still felt as if the gap that had opened between them during their earlier argument was still open and raw, like a wound.

Sure enough, Eileen's kind eyes told her she'd seen through Faith's words. "You'll work it out. I know you will. After all the bumps in the road you two have faced, how can you not?"

Faith wanted to share her aunt's confidence, but she found she couldn't quite make that leap.

19

The arc of expensive sports cars had left the lawn. The fans of Red Maxton, the guests of what was supposed to be his retirement party, had departed. The hedge maze was just another landscape feature on the manor grounds, no longer a crime scene.

There was indeed buzz about the party in the press. After all, the murder of a celebrity secret twin was a story too good to pass up. But the coverage ended up being more about the dramatic and tragic end of Red Maxton's career than Trey Connor's last drive off into the sunset.

The final book was due out in a matter of months. Nick had sent Faith and Wolfe a picture of the cover. It didn't feature Angela's stolen car or Denise. Instead, the cover showed only a dark, stylized silhouette of a man in a tuxedo walking off into the distance. No one could say if the last book in the series would do well or fizzle without Red's dynamic personality to promote it.

The first of the replacement windows had arrived at the cottage. They were propped up against Faith's wall inside their boxes, awaiting installation. Everything was back to normal.

Everything except Faith and Wolfe. He'd been peculiarly distant since that night with the pressure cuffs in the shed. Overly attentive one minute, then polite and procedural the next. Their companionship had been simple and comfortable, but now it seemed to be fraying. While they'd never openly discussed it, Faith's brush with danger had somehow raised the stakes between them, and neither one of them seemed to know whether to move backward or forward.

Faith had come to care deeply for Wolfe. But as Wolfe stood on the cottage patio and awkwardly informed her of his sudden travel plans, she wondered what exactly their relationship had become.

"I'm going to England tomorrow," he announced after a few stiff pleasantries. "Sudden, I know, but something's come up."

"England?" Faith stared at Wolfe.

"London, to be exact," he replied, thrusting his hands into his pockets. "I've spent a lot of time at the manor this spring, and some things need tending over there."

Wolfe traveled extensively, and he had business interests all over the world. In fact, Faith's friends often teased her that Wolfe's recent extended stays at Castleton were proof of his growing affection for her.

This trip shouldn't have surprised or bothered her, but it did. She couldn't help but notice the cooling in his demeanor over the past week. She had no logical reason to find his travel announcement distressing, yet her mind reeled at his sudden plans. She had hoped the trial they'd shared would bring them closer, but apparently that hadn't happened.

When he'd called on her at the cottage this afternoon, she'd been pleased at first. They'd had virtually no time alone together since that horrible night at the shed.

But now as he spoke, his eyes didn't quite meet hers. Instead, his gaze darted around the patio, returning again and again to the windows leaning against the walls.

"I'll be happy to have my windows back," she bumbled, lost for a better response. *I'll be happy to have my Wolfe back too. Where did he go? Is he even coming back?*

"I expect the windows will be installed by the time I return," he said, oddly formal. "I'll be glad to see that done."

"Yes, it'll be nice to put all that behind me." Faith wanted to say "behind us," but she couldn't.

An awkward silence stretched between them.

"We'll all miss you," Faith blurted out. "We've gotten spoiled with you being here so much lately." She turned away for a moment, feeling foolish. They both knew she meant "I" and not "we," but Faith felt she had no right to get possessive of a man like Wolfe Jaxon.

"Who's going to keep you out of trouble while I'm gone?" He probably meant to say it lightly, but it missed the mark.

"There's always Watson," she said with a forced laugh. How had they lost the ease between them that she once treasured? Every conversation lately felt too heavy, each of them measuring their words too carefully. They hardly ever laughed or joked as they used to.

"Trust you to the protection of a cat?" Wolfe asked. "Am I to swallow that as a good security plan for my invaluable manor librarian?"

Even with the compliment of "invaluable," it seemed wrong for him to refer to her in purely professional capacities. She was sure they'd grown close, but had they? Perhaps she'd misread their relationship. Perhaps the shift from their friendship into something more didn't mean the same thing to him as it did to her.

"Well, he is an extraordinary cat," Faith replied with an inward cringe. "A hero, in fact. He helped you save me." Her inner cringe deepened. It didn't feel right to bring that up.

"Yes, he is an extraordinary cat." Wolfe studied Faith for a long moment, and the barest hint of his usual glow returned with his devastating smile. "I will be back."

Faith was surprised at how much she had needed to hear that. There was the tone of a promise in his words, but it never quite reached his eyes. While she had no real reason to, a corner of her heart worried she was about to lose him. If she'd ever really had him. The doubtful part of her heart stilled, waited for him to say something like, "I think we should see other people while I'm gone."

Faith didn't want to see other people. She'd already lost her heart to Wolfe, and she couldn't simply reclaim it. If he really was pulling away from her, then maybe it was good that he was going to London. It would be easier, and she'd still have the steadfast support of her friends and family here.

He didn't say anything else as he stared at her. As if he were committing her features to memory. Or deciding something.

Or saying goodbye without actually saying it.

Faith felt her throat tighten and tears prick her eyes. "Have a wonderful trip," she said, forcing brightness into her voice. "Get lots of business done. We'll carry on here."

"I know you will. It will be a busy summer for you."

That felt like a cryptic remark. Did that mean he'd be gone for weeks or months?

"Busy is always good." Faith wanted to smack her forehead at the awkward words. If this really was goodbye, it was an awful, stumbling one. All the ease of their friendship had vanished, and Faith realized she'd be as heartsick over that loss as much as any romantic break.

"Take care until I return, Faith." Wolfe touched her cheek, then left a tender kiss there as well. The gesture could have been a promise, or it could have been goodbye.

Faith wanted to grab his shoulders and plead that he tell her which, but she couldn't. Willing tears not to come, she simply nodded.

"You too, Watson," Wolfe said, leaning down to give the cat an affectionate stroke.

Watson arched his back to meet Wolfe's hand.

Rumpy had warmed to Wolfe as much as she had, and that almost made it worse.

As Wolfe stepped off the patio and began walking across the lawn, Faith watched his tall frame silhouetted against the summer sun. *Like the final Trey Connor cover*, she thought, which felt far too final. Was his goodbye more permanent than his words?

Watson jumped up to join her, settling on the low patio wall beside her.

"Have I lost him?" she asked aloud.

Neither the summer air nor her cat answered, but she felt Watson nudge up against her. She glanced down at her cat, sure his expression said, "You'll never lose me."

Faith picked Watson up and held him close. "You truly are an extraordinary cat."

He purred loudly as if to say, "I know."

"Your fan club has arrived," Eileen announced.

Faith opened the cottage door to see Midge, Brooke, Eileen, and even Atticus gathered on her front steps the next evening.

"Fan club?" Faith asked with a laugh. "My calendar says this is a book group meeting."

"Oh, it was," Brooke said as she stepped into the living room. "But since a certain someone made last-minute travel plans, we decided we'd make an impromptu switch of plans too."

"We're going to England?" Faith was proud her voice didn't catch on the question.

London had felt halfway around the world as she'd watched Wolfe's car pull out of the driveway earlier that day.

"Heavens no. Something much yummier." Brooke held up a bakery box. "Cheesecake. With three choices of toppings."

Eileen showed Faith a stack of DVDs. "And your choice of six Agatha Christie film adaptations for entertainment. No spy flicks whatsoever."

Midge carried Atticus and a large bag. "Not to mention sparkling juice and some excellent Swiss chocolates. A few goodies for Watson and Atticus too."

Atticus barked a greeting to Watson.

The cat merely raised his head in minimal acknowledgment to the dog.

"Book group can wait. Showing our support for you can't." Eileen handed an envelope to Faith. "Four tickets to a book fair in Boston next weekend. We figured it was time for a girls' getaway."

"What a marvelous idea," Faith replied, gratitude swelling her chest. She glanced at the trove of goodies and amusements before her. "And you're right. This is way better than book club."

Eileen set the DVDs down and gave Faith a hug. "After all, we're more than a book club, aren't we?"

"I don't know what I'd do without you," Faith said with no hope of ignoring the lump rising in her throat.

"Of course you do," Brooke said. "You'd do great. You're intelligent and brave and strong and a whole bunch of other terrific things."

"We're just here to help you over the bumps," Midge said, opening the box of chocolates. "Same as you'd do for us."

Brooke ducked into the kitchen to fetch plates, forks, and glasses. Within minutes, a delicious spread filled Faith's coffee table.

Eileen pointed at the stack of DVDs. "This may end up being a late night. How did you sleep last night?"

"I thought I'd toss and turn after Wolfe's goodbye, but I didn't," Faith admitted. "As a matter of fact, I had the first good night's sleep I've had in ages."

"What do you suppose that means?" Brooke asked.

"It means her body has figured out what her head and heart will know soon enough," Midge responded.

"Which is?" Faith asked.

"That you're going to be fine no matter what Wolfe ends up doing. You've got us, you've got the perfect job at a gorgeous library, you've got Watson"—Midge gestured to the spread—"and you've got a serious amount of goodies here."

Faith met the eyes of each of her dear friends. "I do, don't I?"

"Always have," Eileen said. "Now which will it be first? *Death on the Nile* or *Murder on the Orient Express*?"

"As long as it's not a Trey Connor movie, either one is fine," Faith replied.

Eileen slid *Murder on the Orient Express* into the player as

Midge poured glasses of sparkling juice and Brooke passed around slices of cheesecake.

Faith smiled as she accepted a slice of cheesecake generously doused with raspberry sauce.

"To our Faith," Midge toasted, raising her glass.

"To our Faith," the rest chimed in.

Atticus jumped onto Midge's lap as the movie began.

Within a few minutes, Faith felt Watson snuggle up beside her, his low purring a reassuring comfort.

Faith gazed around the room at her friends and smiled. Life was sure to offer up a new adventure, and she was thankful for her remarkable friends to share it with. It was only a matter of turning the page and watching the next chapter unfold.

Up to this point, we've been doing all the writing. Now it's *your* turn!

Tell us what you think about this book, the characters, the bad guy, or anything else you'd like to share with us about this series. We can't wait to hear from *you*!

Log on to give us your feedback at:
https://www.surveymonkey.com/r/CastletonLibrary

Annie's® FICTION